MY EVER PATHETIC LIFE

Selisa Lyn Johnson

Johnson Global Publishing Group, LLC

JOHNSON GLOBAL PUBLISHING GROUP

The characters and events portrayed in this book are fictitious. Any similarity to real persons, living or dead, is coincidental and not intended by the author.

Cover design by: Art Painter
Library of Congress Control Number: 2018675309
Printed in the United States of America

For information, address River's Edge Press, an imprint of Johnson Global Publishing Group LLC, 4952 S Rainbow BLVD, Ste 150 #1006, Las Vegas, NV 89118

Adrian and Latricia:
I love you both very much, and you two are the only reasons that I took a chance, and I finally decided to get some of my books published. Sometimes, I know I keep putting things off, and I get scared of failing again, but with your encouragement, I am just going to go for it. I know in the past, a lot of times, I've felt like I've fallen short of the mark, and I regret not giving you the perfect lives I had planned. Without you both, I'm all alone, and feeling like the bad times would last forever. I just have to look at the two of you, and for the first time, I honestly believe that I'm smart and that I can do anything I set my mind to. Even if I'm not perfect and nothing ever goes the way I want, you are just happy to have me for a mother. I will always be there for you both, and the bonds between us won't ever break. Sometimes, you can feel like you have gone through so much, and it's just a struggle not to give in to the pain. I guess there are hard life lessons you have to learn. Even if emotionally, you are falling apart and feeling like you are just going to drown in despair. You just have to finally rise above it all and seek inside you the strength to stand on your own two feet and try not to fail anymore.

CONTENTS

RESOURCES

Website	http:// www.selisalynjohnsonbooks.com
Facebook	selisalynbooks
Instagram	selisalynbooks
Twitter	selisalynbooks

SEARCH FOR SELF

From the Fall of 1988 until the Spring of 1990, a group of kids attends Central high school, experiences the struggles of being a teenager. The recent closing of Lincoln High School on the southside of town causes the transfer of over three hundred black students to a dominantly white, Central High School. Making for an even greater need to climb higher up the popularity ladder, just to fit in.

If the cultural clash on both sides wasn't enough, the town's biggest employer, The Mill, laid off hundreds of workers after a big strike. Sometimes, it's like no matter what, nothing ever works out the way you want it to, and you only spend most of your time dealing with everything. The kids in the "Search for Self" series only try to cope with things and not get caught up in all the despair they face.

The series focuses on allowing the reader to become a part of the adventures of various students from all walks of life as they deal with their emotions, friendships, and growth as individuals.

CHAPTER 1

I'm always worrying about proving myself to people. I want to be thought of as exceptional by everyone. I have a lot of doubts about myself, and so it's like I need to prove something to everybody. I'm not too smart, so I need to leave my mark somehow. It's not like I have a chance of being a stand-out by doing something so unusual that it gets me noticed.

Sometimes some of those kids from the good parts of the town come along. Everybody moves out of the way like we can't even touch them, or something will rub off. I know I hate them for getting that kind of respect, but I want to be like that. I play the game, and I talk about the Preps like they're not exceptional, but I know inside I'm dying to be like them.

That's why my biggest dream is to be popular. I see how those kids do things, and I hear about the things they're up to before they get all hush-hush, and they act like if one of us heard, we'd take it away from them. They're probably right. If I had the chance, I'd be doing the same things the Preps do, and who knows? I may act the same way too. You know, like I don't think I'm better than everybody else, but why can't other people think that?

At school, it's like I'm not even there. Central High is a big school, and it's scary in the beginning, but I've tackled the school, and I know my way around pretty well. The only thing I can't get is how to fit in with the right kinds of people. I'm not putting myself down, but I can see how things are.

Like I went into the john the other day, and these two Preps were talking by the sink. One's complaining because her daddy only gave her four hundred dollars that weekend to go shopping. The other one is agreeing that he did her wrong. Shit, I'm thinking, I don't get that much spent on me in a year, and those two bitches are complaining.

You know, I felt like shit in last year's jeans and better- than-nothing-at-all top that Dad brought me just to get me off his case about wanting something new. I acted like the Preps didn't even faze me, though, and I went on into the john to do business. Inside, I was thinking that for once - just one time now – that I could get some of the good things out of life and stop getting kicked in the ass by everybody else.

Maybe that's why I try to do some ass-kicking of my own. Nobody else is going to do it, so I try to look out for myself. People try, but nobody gets the best of me. I dog people out, and I'm on the second punch before they even know what hit them. I take shit around the house all the time, but I'd be damned if I'd let the bastards at school get me down.

You know, sometimes I get carried away, and I really act the ass. I do shit that I think about later, and I'm asking myself why I did it. I don't want to walk on nobody, but if it'll keep me from getting stomped into the ground, that's just how it is.

Lately, I've been trying to control my temper, though, and keep everyone from jumping my shit about how I treat everyone else. My mother says I'm going to run across the wrong person one of these times, and I'm going to get messed up. I don't like admitting it, but I know she's right most of the time. Like you can't keep taking from people all the time before somebody dogs your shit, but you can't give yourself to them either and let them do what they want. I just don't know how to act. Be a giver or a taker; there doesn't seem to be any middle ground.

You know, like I have relaxed a little, but people know I'm still so hip. Nobody gets inside my head unless I want them to, and I don't, so I don't have to worry about getting dogged out. But the thing is, how do you keep from dogging your own self out?

CHAPTER 2

My life is so dull that it's pathetic. Nothing much ever happens to me. I feel like my whole existence is just at a standstill. I'm beginning to think I will never be a part of everything at school, and my home life is the pits. The Preps rule at my school. I'm nothing like them. My parents act like I'm such a bother, and I know they would rather not deal with me. I want to be popular so bad, but I don't want to change everything about me. I know things will get worse before they get any better at home, so I don't have any hope of things improving between my parents and me. I feel like everything that goes on in my life is a lost cause, and I will never be able to figure it all out.

Mostly, I'm just trying to make it through each new day. It's such a hassle being a teenager, and it's especially hard being at a school like Central. It's like the rich kids rule there, and the rest of us don't stand a chance. There's no way I'll ever have enough money to buy my way in at school, so I'll have to find another way to get in with the popular kids. I'm not a loser or anything, but I'm not a big winner either. I guess I'm just somewhere in the middle.

Things are just a certain way at school, and the popular kids know how to make you feel like you don't fit in. They go around like they own Central, and it's like the rest of us are just there. I look at the top kids at school, and I know I want to be just like them. Getting all that respect and having everybody act like I'm so special. For once, I want to feel like I'm even essential, and I want to believe I matter. A lot of times, I feel like I'm just invisible, and nobody barely notices me.

I know I'm not the only one who has things bad. It's like most of the kids at school are outsiders like me, and it's like there's no way we will ever be "in." Those kids from the southside of town just stand around and only hang out with each other, and I know they have it even worse. There were always about thirty-five black kids at Central, but last spring Lincoln High School was closed, and about three hundred of those kids have been bused to Central. I'm happy there are so many black kids at school, but it's like most of the kids don't want to be bothered with them. I guess the black kids know those kids feel that way about them, and that's why they don't try to associate with us.

Carsonville is so small anyway, and we barely even have any blacks here, and most of them are stuck on the southside of town. Only about five or six black families have moved to the other parts of Carsonville, so nobody really had a chance to associate with all those kids before now. I thought it would be a worthwhile experience to have so many black kids at Central, and I thought it would give everybody a chance to get to know each other. I thought that was the whole point in having them there; for us to hang out together and try to be friends. I don't know why everybody acts like they can't get along, and I wish something would happen to change all that.

Sometimes, it's like our town is separated from the rest of the United States, and nobody even knows we exist. Practically nothing out of the ordinary ever happens here, but it's like everybody is always in everybody else's business. A lot of the stuff that goes on in the big cities doesn't affect us. Some things like drugs do filter through. I have my own thoughts and opinions, and I feel totally different than everybody else around me. It's hard living in a State like Indiana in a small town like Carsonville because nobody else really has a clue, and sometimes I feel like such an outsider.

I try to keep up with the latest trends and know what's going on in the outside world. That's hard because my dad is so cheap with his money, and we don't even have Basic Cable. He's just like that, and it doesn't mean he doesn't make a decent amount of money. He's an Insurance Man at Forrester Insurance, and he must know what he's doing or else he wouldn't have held that job for my whole life. Dad doesn't want Mom working, so she spends most of her time around the house, cleaning up and keeping her eye on Diane and me.

I don't get along with my parents, and I probably never will. They are never there for me, and they are way too strict. I can't do anything without hearing Dad's mouth about it, and he acts like he has to make my life as miserable as possible. Sometimes, I think my parents are so out of it because they're so old. Mom is forty- seven, and Dad is fifty-three. I worry that my parents are so stuck in their ways and that there's no hope of changing them into the kinds of parents I wish I had. I used to talk things over with Diane before she became such a bitch. She shared my opinion of the situation. Lately, I'll be lucky if Diane even acknowledges my existence because she tries to ignore me most of the time.

I spend most of my time plotting about how to get in with the popular kids at school. Sometimes, I think it is hopeless trying to break into any of the influential cliques, but I don't want to give up. I'm pretty, and I have a good personality, and I've been trying to act friendly towards everybody else at school. It's just hard not to get pissed off at particular people, and I struggle with my temper because most of the time, in the past, I've let it get out of control.

I don't want to let everybody just walk all over me. Everybody knows I'm so aggressive, and everybody knows not to bother with me. Still, there's always somebody who will try to test you. I haven't gotten into any fights in high school so far, but all through grade schooland middle school, I had to do battle almost every week. I know it's only a matter of time before somebody comes into my face starting some shit now, and I'll have to stomp their ass to put them back in their place. Sometimes, it's like I can't control myself, and I just want to hurt somebody terribly. I wouldn't even worry about the consequences. I'm just like that. Everybody knows about my reputation for fighting so much. If they start some shit with me anyway, then they deserve what they get.

My middle school Counselor tried to get my parents to send me to Therapy to work on my anger issues. Still, Dad wouldn't do it, and he just said a good ass beating by him would help the situation. That's his answer about everything. Sometimes, I think I'm so aggressive because of the way he always treats me. Diane gets the same lousy treatment, and she floats along in a daze, so I don't know. I really wish I could still talk to my sister about things like that, but we've been this distance with each other for five years, and I know she could care less about how I feel about anything.

It's hard to be a forceful person and just concentrate on doing what it takes to make sure I come out of this whole miserable time in my life with as few scars as possible. It's 1988, and I'm a freshman at Central High School, and I want to make my mark there. I'm tired of harping on all the negative stuff in my life, and I just want to think about something positive for a change. Some things will never change, so I wish to focus on everyday teenage stuff.

I know I really want to be accepted at school and I wish I could do more things to have fun. It's just hard keeping other bad feelings away. My biggest problem is getting my cheap-ass father to put out enough money to get me some decent clothes to wear to school. There's always the reliable lay-a-way, but I get tired of getting my clothes after everybody else has had their clothes for weeks. Nothing will ever change. I might as well get used to my lame existence. It's not like anything exciting is ever going to happen to make my life feel totally terrific for once.

CHAPTER 3

I have two good friends. Jody Travis is my best friend. We don't have that many interests we share, but she's lots of fun to be around, and I know she's there for me when I need her. Mark Davis is in a lot of my classes, and we're always joking around. He seems to trust me with his personal business, so he shares a lot of stuff about his girlfriend with me. Even If I got accepted, I would want to remain friends with them.

Gale Stewart says she's my friend too, but sometimes I really doubt that. She's not around half the time, and when she is, all she talks about is herself. Gale is popular. I think that is really the only reason I put up with her. She is very dull to listen to, and she tries to talk about Jody and me so much. I laugh it off a lot, but one of these times, she's going to catch me off guard, and I'm going to pop her in her big mouth.

Everybody at school talks about Gale, but we still act friendly in her face. She's only been at Central for a couple of months, but she knows practically everybody there. When she manages to give Jody and me some of her time, all she talks about is what she does with the older crowd her sister, Tracey, belongs to. According to her, all she does is party all the time. Gale has a different date every night.

She makes me feel left out. Jody doesn't like Gale, and she says that she doesn’t care what she does, but I wish I had a big sister who did something like get me in with the right kids at school, so I could be as popular as Gale is. I wouldn't mind having all the money she has either. Her father is President of the Carsonville Bank. Gale gets a big allowance. She's always buying me Cokes and stuff, but I don't try to take advantage of her. I try to like Gale for herself, not because the girl is free with her money. The thing about Gale is that she loves stealing and it doesn't matter how much money she always has in her pockets because she does it all the time. Gale tried to make me seem chicken when I wouldn't go shopping that way with her. Popularity doesn't mean me getting myself into serious trouble. I don't care how much stuff I want, I'm not going to stoop to stealing like a dummy to get it. I guess that's why Gale hasn't asked me to go to the Strip Mall with her lately, and she's been so distant since I turned her down last week. It doesn't matter, because her stealing just gives people more stuff to talk about her over and she already gets enough of that about how she treats the guys that she dates.

I used to feel sorry for Gale. I know a lot of guys

and to hear them talk, you'd think that she's been with every one of them. She goes on a lot of dates, and all of them say they score with her. I'm beginning to believe them. Gale carries on with guys in the halls at school, and if that's what she does in public, I'd hate to see what she does in private. Gale's only a freshman, and already she's known around school as the easiest girl there. Guys laugh and joke around about her dropping her drawers for a Big Mac and a Shake. Gale is pretty, and she can afford anything she could ever want, and Gale shouldn't have to take shit off nobody, so I don't know why she sells herself so cheap.

Jody is the opposite of her. She gives guys the deep freeze, and nobody can get through. She got asked out by Tony Phillips, but she turned him down. Tony is famous, and he's supposed to be influential. You don't turn a guy like that down. Girls know how things are around here, and there are these guys you are just supposed to date because it's expected of you because they can make or break you socially. Since then, no other guys have tried to ask her out. I bet they figure if she turned Tony down, then none of them have a chance because they think she is so stuck-up on herself, and they don't want to be bothered with her. Jody is the most beautiful girl at our whole school, and she gets a lot of attention from guys. She acts like it's all a big bore. Whenever I try to talk to her about guys, she behaves like she's not interested, and I wonder to myself if maybe she's a dyke. Still, I don't really want to know the answer, because I like having her as a friend.

Jody is not accepted either. She stays at home too much. When I want to do something, I need to force her to go. Her parents don't have her on a curfew, but she always goes home when I do. I tell her she should be out trying to have fun and trying to make an impression on the kids at school. Still, Jody refuses to do anything that will help her popularity. Sometimes, I worry about that girl, and I know it's going to have to be up to me to get us involved in things.

Jody seems to go out of her way to be different. I would like to stand out too, but you need to follow along with the crowd on some things. You don't want to be weird. If you go out of your way to be different than everyone else, then they're not going to ask you to do anything with them. You need to pretend that you have things in common. She may be beautiful and all that, but sometimes you need to make an effort to belong, or kids aren't going to think you fit in with them, and then where is she going to be? Jody said she wants the kids at school to accept her the way she is, and if they can't, then it's just too bad.

I can't understand her. I'm trying to figure out ways to get us involved at Central. I get tired of just taking up space and hearing how much fun the other kids are having. We haven't done anything at all this year, and we don't belong to any clubs or activities. I feel like the only kids besides Gale who we even talk to are just like us, and we are almost scraping the bottom of the barrel. We're not really losers, but we're not exactly living a carefree teenage existence either and having everything go our way. I don't want to be a "straight" for the next four years. That's what they call the kids who don't do the things the other kids do. I really want to fit in and be a part of stuff. It's no fun getting left out. I'm not content to stay on the sidelines. I have to be in on things that the other kids are involved in, or I'll never feel like I'm essential and a regular teenager. Most of the time, I feel so separated from the big happenings at school, and I stay so jealous of the kids in the spotlight. I never get to do anything, and my life is so dull that it's even more pathetic than I thought.

I want some excitement in my life. I'm tired of sitting at home every night. There are so many things that are happening. Carsonville is so small, and things seem dead most of the time, but the right kids know how to find fun out there. I hear some of the kids talking about the parties they go to, and they talk about the other exciting things they do. I haven't even been to Cassidy's on Friday or Saturday night when it's the teen place to hang out. Or went cruising on Green River Road like Gale does every weekend with her sister and Tracey's best friend, Marie Hopkins. Shit, I don't get to go nowhere. I feel left out. Going to high school isn't any fun if the only thing you do is attend classes. There are so many other fascinating things to do, but if things don't change soon, I'll never be a part of it.

Maybe to some people being popular doesn't

matter. Like to Jody. She says that she doesn't care about being accepted. She says that she would be happy to have a few kids to hang around, and the numbers don't matter because that many kids can't really get to know you well and form any lasting friendships. She wants people to really like her. I want the same thing myself, but I want people to look up to me too. I never get treated like I'm exceptional at home, so I want to get some attention from the other kids at school. Is that too much to ask for?

I don't get along with my sister, Diane. She's three years older than me, and we used to be cool, but after she turned into a teenager four years ago, she became a bitch, and we haven't gotten along ever since then. I thought when I turned thirteen that she would be like how Tracey does Gale and take me under her wings to teach me things, but that bitch could care less about me, and I'm left out in the cold. Diane is popular. She belongs to a lot of clubs and stuff, and she used to be smart in school before she ran away from home, and then Diane changed into a different person when she finally got back home. When I showed up at Central, a lot of my teachers expected me to be just like her. I can't tell you how many times I've heard, "You're Diane Moore's sister, aren't you? She was an excellent student, and freshman year, she really stood out." I don't need Diane's achievements thrown up in my face. I get enough of that at home.

My parents think she can't do anything wrong, and even when she ran away, they blamed the guy she was with, and they acted like Diane was innocent, and he was the big problem. I'm always hearing how perfect she is. I can't do anything wrong without hearing about it for fifty years. Still, my parents can't remember a single thing she's ever done to disappoint them, and they don't want to hear it when I try to throw the shit up in their faces. I can't do anything to measure up, so I don't even try anymore, because who really wants to keep getting rejected and treated as if they're nothing at all? I know my parents love her more than me, and it's all because she's adopted. They feel like they need to make her feel special, and they never stop to think about what that does to me. They never give me any attention no matter what I do, and they act like they wish I wasn't even around half the time. My parents behave like it's this burden doing what little they do for me. Diane acts like she doesn't want to be bothered with my parents most of the time, and they go out of their way to be decent to her.

I'm their biological daughter, and they ignore me. I could do anything wrong I want, and I could get away with it, like drinking. Where else could I live and regularly drink for over four years and not have my parents notice? They can be so dumb. They're always throwing Diane up in my face, and she's a doper. Diane can't get through the day without getting high. Diane's up first thing every morning smoking some weed. The only way she gets away with being high at school is because everyone likes her. She can talk so dumb. I mean that both ways. What she says is dumb, and she sounds dumb. I'm supposed to look up to Diane and want to be just like her. Well, Mom and Dad, you got your wish because every little problem I have, I get out the bottle, and lately, that's been a hell of a lot. You want me to be so much like Diane, and you're always pushing her in my face and telling me I should be just like her, so I'll have my little addiction too. I guess you'll never even figure that out because you're so busy thinking Diane's so perfect and doing everything to please her that you never even notice me. Sometimes, I get so mad at that bitch, and I hate the fact that she is my sister.

We get into a lot of fights. I get mad because Diane has things so easy, and I'll say something to get on her nerves. She treats me like I'm nothing, and most of the time, she doesn't say anything to me at all. When her friends are around, Diane tries to put me down in front of them, making me feel like a stupid kid. At school, she acts like I don't exist, and she can walk past me like she doesn't even see me. That's okay. I'm not going to kiss her stupid ass just to make her like me and have her accept me as her sister, so we can be close like we were when we were kids. When she didn't know she was adopted yet and hate me because I couldn't be special like her. I don't need her to be a great sister like Tracey, and I'm not going to beg her for a little of her time, and she can just keep Mom and Dad wrapped around her finger. I've been at Central for a couple of months, and I'm learning the ropes. Who even needs her? I'm tough as nails, and I'll find my own way to make it, and I'll be just fine.

Since I can't get the attention I want at home, I try to get it at school. I know there is no way that my parents will ever change, so I've stopped trying to get some attention from them. What's the use of putting yourself out for people who just act like you're wasting their time and always make you feel like you're not even worthwhile? Sometimes, I think they don't love me at all. I'm not going to go out of my way to get hurt by them. They've put me through enough shit, and I've suffered all the pain I'm going to because you can only beat down a dog so much before she learns to avoid your fists. The best thing they can do for me is just to leave me alone.

CHAPTER 4

Jody and I are on the way to her house. This is the first time that she's invited me over. I can't wait to meet Jody's folks. She talks about them all the time, and they seem terrific. I guess I figure anybody who has parents who try to understand them, and they don't give them hassles about the slightest thing have things made as far as I'm concerned.

I talk a lot to cover up for Jody's silence. She never talks that much, but she seems fidgety, and it's like her mind is far off. I guess she's worried about introducing me to her parents. I can understand that. You never know what they'll do. I would hate for her to spend any time around Mom and Dad. Dad is always gruff, and Mom is overly nice.

When Diane's friends come over, Mom hangs around the room, and she laughs a lot, and it's like she wants to fit in with them. I know Diane wishes she would act her age. Mom gets silly, and she says stupid stuff. I don't understand why Mom does that. It seems idiotic to me, and she embarrasses us. I know if I feel like that if she does it to Diane's friends, I'd really feel bad if it was my friends.

"My sister put ketchup on the cat and ate him," I say to shake Jody up.

"She did?"

"Jody, what's wrong with you?" I ask. "I just told you Diane ate the cat, and you act like that's normal."

"I wasn't listening."

"I can see that," I say. "Why are you acting so funny?"

"I was thinking about my parents. You know how parents are."

Jody makes a puking gesture, and she crosses her eyes.

"I know what you mean."

"Here's my house."

We go up a walk to this giant house. Those two blocks really make a big difference. Jody's house is sizable than any other dwelling in the entire neighborhood, and it really stands out. I figure somebody had to have it specially made because all the other houses are just the same. The only thing different is the color of their shutters. There's a huge yard out front, and I bet they have a big backyard, too. Somebody has taken a lot of trouble to get the front yard in shape, and it looks like a miniature forest. I guess they want their privacy, because the house is hidden behind all these shrubs, and you can't just get the full impact from the street. Jody takes out her key, and she unlocks the door.

"Come on in."

Jody must be rich. I can tell by the way her house is furnished. Everything is perfect, and nothing is out of place. I would never have believed it. She acts like a normal kid whose parents have a regular income, and she told me that her dad was a mechanic. I'd like to know why Jody feels like she needs to lie if she was sitting on all this money and living this good. She's not snobbish, and she doesn't have her nose out of joint. I would think I'm "Ms. It." I bet all their furniture is expensive and everything looks so new.

"Angel, you look like you just died and went to heaven."

"What can I say?" I ask. "This is pretty nice."

"It's only stuff."

"Of course, you can say that," I tell her. "You're used to it."

"Not really," she says. "Do you want a Pepsi?"

"Sure. Do you mind if I sit down?"

"Go right ahead," she says. "I should have told you to."

Jody goes into the kitchen, and I sit down on the sofa. It's not like it is when you sit on our couch. It's soft and cushiony. When you sit on our couch, you can feel a spring sticking in your ass. I'm really impressed with everything. Jody probably thinks I'm not used to the expensive stuff. I'm not, but I don't want her to know that. I get my composure back together, and I start acting like I'm not so impressed with everything.

"Where did you live before you came to Carsonville?" I ask curiously.

Jody only moved to town about two weeks before school started, and her family's business hasn't gotten broadcast yet. I know I'm being nosy, but that doesn't stop me from wanting to know something about Jody. I guess it comes from living in small towns all my life and knowing at least a little something about the people who live around me.

"All over, I mean, when I was little, we traveled a lot, and then we settled down in New York."

"That sounds great. I wish I could do that. We lived in Vicksburg until about five years ago. I've never even been out of Indiana before."

"Well, I don't really remember all that traveling," she says. "Just when we lived in New York."

"It must have been nice," I say. "The thing I can't imagine is somebody leaving an exciting place like New York to come to a boring place like Carsonville."

"New York is okay, I guess, but my mom wanted to be near her folks. She grew up here, but she hadn't been back since I was born."

"Who would want to come back here? Mostly, everyone is out to finish school and leave town. The stupid ones get a job at the Mill, and they get stuck here all their lives."

"My grandfather is a Supervisor at the Mill. I guess it's the biggest employer in town, isn't it? He talks a lot about the Strike, and he said if it's up much longer, the Owners might sell the Plant, and a lot of people would lose their jobs. It would probably hurt the town a lot. My mom said the township has really grown since the Mill expanded. It draws a lot of people to Carsonville. "

"But working there is such a drag. How exciting could it be going there eight hours a day doing the same thing every day? That's why when I'm out of school, I'm getting as far away from this town as I can, and I'm never looking back."

"You say that now, but you'll probably change your mind. Nobody is forcing people to stay. I haven't lived here that long, but I like it. You can see how much the town has changed. The closer you get to downtown, the more you can see how things used to be. My mother was so shocked when we first got back here. Two shopping malls and all those apartments on the East side of town. I was expecting some little place that had nothing going for it except the gossip, and we find this. I really like it here now, but when we first moved here, I was determined to hate it."

"I can understand that, coming here from New

York."

"Hey, do you want to go up to my room and listen to some music?"

"Okay, why not?"

The stairs have thick beige carpeting. When you take a step, your feet sink down. It's not the same as the stuff on our floors. Jody's room is pink and white. Everything matches. The curtains are striped, and they match the canopy over the bed and the bedspread. The walls are painted white, and they match the carpeting. There's a stereo with an enormous stack of records, and a color TV which I bet has Cable. There's a computer on her desk, and Jody even has her own phone. I bet Jody gets everything she wants. No wonder she doesn't worry about living in our stupid town. I guess I wouldn't either if I got spoiled rotten.

"Wow! What a perfect room for a girl."

"You think so? I hate it. Barfy pink and white. The only thing mine is the bean bag chair."

Talk about barfy. This beat-up green bean bag chair is in the corner. Jody goes over to her stereo, and she puts a record on. I sit on her bed, and she comes towards me. She sits next to me.

If I had a room like this, I'd have a slumber party or something. It would really impress the girls at school. I could always have friends over for Cokes and everything. I bet Jody's parents would go out of their way to make her friends feel at home. If I had parent go-ahead and a room like this, I would be super popular.

"Wouldn't it be great to be popular?" I ask. "Getting asked out on a date every weekend. Joining a lot of clubs and being involved in so many activities. Being a Cheerleader or maybe becoming a Honey Bear."

"It's funny, but I don't even want to become popular."

"I think every girl wants to be popular."

"Not me. I'd die if a bunch of popular kids started talking to me. Not that there's any danger of that happening."

"I'd love to be a part of things at school."

"Me too," Jody says. "Like on the Basketball Team."

"I'm not trying out for any contact sports. I don't need any reason for people to call me a dyke."

"They don't do that."

"Yes, they do," I say. "Diane said..."

"Since when did you start listening to Diane?"

"I don't." I signal that I'm not finished talking, and then I take a sip of my Pepsi. "But she knows about things like this."

"I still want to try out," she says. "Maybe get a Letter Sweater."

"All right," I say in a voice of dire prediction.

"I said, try out."

"You're not in Gym class. You don't know what it's like. Diane says it's a lot worse when you shower with the jocks."

"Suzy probably wouldn't let me anyway."

"Who's Suzy?"

"She's my mom."

"You call your mother by her first name?"

"Sure, why not?"

I have a thousand reasons why not, but I can see that Jody doesn't want to make a big deal about it. I would never call Mom or Dad by their names. They would think I was being disrespectful towards them, and I'd get a slap from Dad about it.

"It seems strange to me," is all I say.

"I guess I'm just used to it."

"I wonder what makes it happen?"

"What?"

"Getting to be popular at school and having all the kids like you."

"I don't know," she says. "I wish I knew."

I think about it. It's not like Jody and myself are a couple of losers. I wouldn't be nobody's choice for

Homecoming Court, but I'm pretty enough. You don't have to be smart either. Gale is in a lot of the hard classes that Jody is in, but she's about the dumbest person I know. Besides, I have a good personality, and I'm not lacking in confidence. I sure wish I knew that answer.

"The only thing really wrong with us is that we're too nice," Jody sums up the whole situation.

"Don't I know that?"

Gale is fun, and she's frank, but nobody would call her nice. She's out for herself, and she only looks out for number one. A lot of the popular kids that I know are friendly enough when they want something, but mostly they ignore us unfortunate ones. I wouldn't call any of them nice. I'm moody sometimes, but I don't go out of my way to be mean to anybody. I treat people the way I want to be treated. Maybe I should change that. Who wants to be thought of as nice? I'd rather be anything but.

"Jody! I'm home."

I can hear Jody's mom coming up the stairs. I wonder what she'll think about me. Maybe she'll wonder why her daughter chose somebody like me to be her friend. With a house decorated like hers and everything, I know they really have a lot of money, and I wonder if she'll be snobbish. They don't live in an uppity neighborhood, but everything about the house spells rich. Her mother enters the room, and I just stare at her. I can't believe it. Jody's mom is black!

CHAPTER 5

I sit there staring at her like a dummy, and I feel like every fool in the book. I bet she thinks I've never even seen a black person before, and I hope she doesn't think I'm a bigot or something. I just wanted to make a good impression on Jody's mother, and now I'm worried that I've proved how stupid I am, and she'll think I don't even deserve to be Jody's friend. It takes only about ten seconds for my brain to return to normal. Still, I know Jody's mother saw how shocked I was. Especially since my mouth fell open and my eyes got big like they do when somebody catches me by surprise. I try to act like everything is okay and that I'm not shocked by the whole situation.

"What have you two been up to?" she covers for me. "I wanted to be here when you came home, but I had to stay after school for one of my classes."

"Uh, it's good to meet you - uh, Mrs. Travis," I manage.

"It's Ms. Are you two getting along okay?"

We nod.

I watch Jody's mother. I'm not staring with cow eyes, but I watch her. She seems too young to be the mother of a daughter Jody's age. She's dressed casually in jeans and a gray Carsonville State University tee shirt, and she appears relaxed. She doesn't seem to be going out of her way to be friendly towards me. It's like she's really interested. I bet I'm not going to have any more trouble talking to her. I don't feel so uptight about her being a grownup, and she knows how to make you relax. Her mother doesn't have the same effect on Jody. She's staring at the wall, and she's not saying anything at all.

"How about having dinner with us, Angel?" her mom asks. "Then, Tom can drive you to the football game from here."

"I'll have to ask my mother."

"Give me your answer after you do."

Her mom leaves the room, and Jody looks towards me. I don't know what's wrong with her. She can't be embarrassed about her mother. I would love to have a mother who could talk to me. Mom tries too hard. Either she's trying to be my best friend or else she doesn't give me any attention at all.

"I'll call my mother now."

"You don't have to do that."

"Don't you want me to stay?" I ask. "Either you do, or you don't."

"Okay, I do."

I go over to the phone, and I dial home. Mom asks a lot of questions, but she finally says I can stay. I tell Jody the news, and she acts like she wished Mom had said "no" or something. I can't understand her. Jody said that she wanted me to stay, so why is she acting so weird?

"I'll go tell Suzy."

I go over to the stereo, and I put on another record. About twenty minutes pass. I flip through the albums, so I'll have something to do. I don't know what the big deal is. It shouldn't take that long to tell your mother that your friend is going to have dinner with you. Jody finally comes back into the room, and she looks like she's been crying. If I had known she would get this upset, I would have never agreed to stay.

"What's wrong, Jody?" I ask.

"Nothing, I'm just crazy. I was so ashamed of my parents."

"Ashamed about what?" I ask. "Being adopted isn't such a big deal."

"That's not it. I'm not adopted. Is that what you thought? Suzy is my real mother."

"That's impossible," I say. "You two hardly look

alike."

"I take after my father."

"Why didn't you tell me your parents have a mixed marriage?"

"Because they don't..."

"But you just said..."

"No, I didn't. I said I take after my father. My parents aren't married. They live together."

"What!"

"It's not such a big deal."

"Not such a big deal? Why didn't you tell me?"

"I didn't want to be rejected."

"Rejected? Why would I do that? I think it's great."

"Really?"

"Yeah, you have all the excitement. Nothing ever happens with my folks."

"I didn't think you'd take it this well," she says. "I would have told you ages ago if I had known."

"I wish you would have." I look at her. "One question, though. Why aren't your parents married? You're fourteen. That seems like a heck of a long time to live together."

"They love each other. My parents don't need a piece of paper telling them how things are."

"It must be weird," I say. "Not having your parents married, I mean."

"It is. Tom and Suzy can just walk away. No divorce."

"But at least you know they're not sticking together out of formality. If your parents have been together this long, I bet they're never breaking up."

"I hope not. Can we change the subject? I feel guilty."

"Why? This is so interesting."

"Because of the way I treated Suzy," she says sadly. "She really got hurt."

"She probably understands," I say. "Parents understand about things like that."

"Maybe, I've never tried to talk to her about how I feel about their relationship."

"Why not? She seems like she would understand."

"That's the problem. Suzy always understands. I could do anything, and she'd understand."

"You're lucky," I say. "I wish my mother tried to understand me."

I've always wanted that, but Mom always puts me on the defensive. She's the parent, and so she's forever right. Mom doesn't try to see my point of view. She just scolds. That's why I never try to tell her how

I'm feeling or make her understand how hurt I get about the way they treat me because I know she'd never understand. Maybe she wouldn't even try to.

"You wouldn't feel like that if you were always spilling your guts out, and you expected your mom to yell at you, but all she does is talk to you about it. Sometimes, I feel like screaming, 'Suzy, hit me! Yell at me! Anything! Just don't give me that understanding look and soothe things over with kind words!' Sometimes, I bait her just to get an negative reaction out of her, but nothing comes of it. Maybe I'm crazy or something. A lot of kids wish they had a good relationship with their parents. It drives me crazy sometimes."

"I wish we could trade places."

"You don't know what it's really like. I'm not knocking our relationship or anything like that. Still, sometimes I need the stern, scolding parent - not the friend and closest confidant. Suzy and I are closer than any mother and daughter that I know, but I get weird sometimes. I yell at Suzy about stupid things, and I'm really a bitch, and she doesn't get mad. The only time was when I got shitty with her mother, and I was going to go off on her."

"You? You hardly say two sentences without running out of things to say. Today is really the first time you've talked this much."

"You just don't know me. Around here, I talk up a storm, and when I get mad, I really speak my mind."

"You should try that at school, and then Linda wouldn't be on your case all the time."

"She's not even worth getting upset over. Besides, I freeze up at school. I can't help it. I can know what to say and everything, but I can't have a simple conversation with anyone."

"You can talk to me, okay."

"That's because I trust you. I feel like I could tell you anything and you wouldn't think that I was a nut. I sound so stupid to myself sometimes, and I can imagine what everyone else would think."

"I guess it's difficult being shy."

"I'm not really shy - oh, I don't know how to explain it. Suzy gets on me about it all the time. She tries to build up my confidence, and she's full of advice, but saying something and doing it are two different things."

"You're lucky to have a mother so young," I say. "I guess that's why you get along so well."

"I guess so. Suzy's twenty-nine, but sometimes you'd think she was about our age. Suzy likes to share in on the things I do at school and stuff, and sometimes it's like she's more my friend than my mother."

"She must have been pretty young when you were born," I say. "My mom's almost forty-eight."

"Suzy was only fifteen, and sometimes I get to thinking about all she's missed out on because of me, and I wonder if I was worth it. I'm nothing to brag about, and she was put through a lot of shit when she got pregnant with me. It was bad enough that she made love to my father, but to get pregnant with his bastard - you can figure out how that went down."

"You shouldn't call yourself that. That is so stupid. It doesn't matter if your parents weren't married. People make mistakes all the time, and in your case, it wasn't even a mistake. They loved each other, and so you're a part of that love. That's why it's stupid of you to call yourself a bastard."

"I know that, but I hear the kids at school talking about their parents, and I feel funny thinking about how they would feel if they knew about Tom and Suzy. How do you explain that your parents just live together?"

"What's to explain? It's nobody's business except yours. I shouldn't have pried earlier. I wasn't trying to make a big deal about it. I was just curious."

"I wasn't talking about you. I know where your head is at. I meant other people. They could really turn it into something dirty, and I would really hate it if that would happen."

"I don't know what to say. Now, I can understand why you said you didn't want to come back to Carsonville. The town has gotten bigger, but the gossip is just as strong. You really can't do anything in this town without rumors flying."

"My grandfather said something like that. People had told him we were back in town before Suzy had even gotten around to seeing him. That's why I can't understand why it hasn't gotten to school."

"Maybe it isn't such a big deal. Gale said that she goes cruising with some of the older girls, and they go to the southside of town. She said they just talk to the guys, but knowing Gale, she's done a lot more. None of the other white girls have come out in the open and admitted that they're hot for a black guy except for Sheila Haskle, but they aren't fooling anybody. Why should it be any different the other way around?"

"I know that," she says. "That's just how I felt."

"If somebody starts some shit with you, just show them you're proud of your parents. You said you know how to go off on somebody."

"I'm just so stupid. Remember when I said I was ashamed of my parents? What I'm ashamed of is me. They've been put through so much shit, and they've survived, but I'm the little coward. I always act like a nice white girl who lives down the street. I don't own up to who I am. Or show people that I have just as many guts as my parents. That I'm happy that I'm made the way I am, and there's nothing that they say is going to change that."

"Why are you so hard on yourself? Everybody keeps something about themselves secret. It's hard opening yourself up to everyone and having them put you down. I know how you feel."

"Oh, sure, you do. Nothing ever hurts you. And even if you were me, you still wouldn't act as stupidly. If somebody comes up in your face with some shit, you always tell those idiots where to go. Besides, nobody is stupid enough to jump bad with you in the first place. You've got half the school scared to death of you, and the other half have heard about all the fights you got into at middleschool and how you tried to really hurt people, so they're not going to start nothing with you either."

"You can be too tough to mess with too. You just need to have a reputation. By now, everybody figures that you're Goody Two Shoes Jody, and they can do anything to you. You stuck that label on yourself, but that doesn't mean you have to take shit off people. If you loved your parents as much as you say you do, you're not going to let anybody put them down. My parents don't care anything about me, and I'm beginning to feel the same way about them too. Still, that doesn't mean I'd let anybody else talk about them. I'd defend Diane too. Most people are just a bunch of talk anyway."

"I hear what you're saying, and it's not really that I'm scared, but I've never stood up to anybody. I'm like a mouse caught in a trap, and I've got the cheese, but where is my freedom? You know what the crazy thing is? I wish I hadn't turned out looking the way I do. Ever since I can remember, I've wished that I had turned out darker. If it showed, there would be no problem about being mixed, and I could really be like Suzy. We really look a lot alike, but people act like they can't see it. It's this big hang-up I have. Tom is always getting on me about it. He loves me as much as Suzy, and he's not trying to push me out of the nest, but he wants me to find my own separate identity. You know, like try my own wings. It's been just the three of us for so long, and he's worried that I'm too dependent on them. I am trying a little to shake things up, but I'm not really breaking away. I've been going out more and everything, but I don't think I'll ever really be so independent that I don't lean on them for something."

"You're too close to your parents, and I'm barely on speaking terms with mine. I'd do anything to have the kind of relationship you have with your parents with Mom and Dad. At least your parents care about you, and you know they love you. I haven't thought my parents loved me for a long time. Mostly, they don't want to be bothered with me, and they act like they wish I wasn't even around, because all their love is for Diane. All I get is put-downs and pushed around a lot."

"I can't believe that. You sound like your parents are horrible. I bet you're exaggerating. No parents could be that bad."

"Just spend the night over to my house sometimes. You'd see what they're like. If my father talks to me at all, it's to yell at me about my latest mistake. My mother is only happy to see me when it's time to clean up. At least she thinks I'm good for something. Free labor."

"I wish I could stay all night with you, but I've never slept away from home. Maybe you could spend the night over here sometimes."

"Maybe."

"Hey! Jody, Angel! Dinner's ready!" Suzy calls up the stairs.

I can't believe we talked that long. It was our first serious conversation, and I bet we've learned more about each other today than a lot of people learn in their entire friendships. I don't feel funny about telling stuff to Jody anymore. She's good to talk to, and I know she wouldn't spread the things I tell her around the school. Besides, she seems to respect my opinion. It makes me feel good because I know Jody is smarter than me.

At dinner, I meet Jody's father, Tom. He is gorgeous. He has long, sandy brown hair and brown eyes. His cheekbones are terrific, and he has a fantastic smile. He's only wearing cutoffs and a t-shirt, so I can tell that he's built well. If I was older, I could go for him in a big way. Both her parents tell me to call them Tom and Suzy. I guess they make a good couple because her mother is pretty too. I can understand why Jody turned out so beautiful. The dining room is formal, but they don't dress that way. I just feel like the house, and all of its furnishings are just there to show that they are just an ordinary stuffed up family. They're nothing like that at all because they are really laid back.

I don't have any trouble talking to them. We laugh, and we joke at the table. I find out that Jody tells them practically everything she does. Like how she got so sick after I had her sneak two beers out of her refrigerator last Monday morning before school for us to drink. And how she got choked when I convinced her to smoke a cigarette when we were waiting for my dad to pick us up at Northland Mall. I worry at first about her parents thinking I'm a negative influence on Jody and them not wanting her to hang out with me anymore. I know my own parents would get madder than hell if they knew half the stuff I do. I sure wouldn't get away with it, but Tom and Suzy are so cool about everything. They don't even let the things Jody does get to them or worry that I'm leading her down the wrong path. I guess if my parents were younger, I would get understood like that too, but they're a lot older than most of the parents I know, and they're old-fashioned. I don't think they'll ever change, so I've stopped hoping that they ever will.

CHAPTER 6

I have been walking around Cassidy's with Jody for the past half hour. I almost had a heart attack when Dad said I could come here after the football game. Usually, he doesn't want me to go anywhere. Gale doesn't ask me to go anywhere with her anymore. She said, "Your father will come to get you in two hours." That's true. Every time I get into the middle of having fun, I need to call him to pick me up.

Well, I'm going to have fun while I can. I think I look cute and sexy, bouncing along in my tight jeans and revealing tee-shirt. I have a fantastic shape, and I like showing it off. The guys seem to appreciate it, and I get a lot of comments. I don't mind cracks from guys. It makes me feel like I'm pretty, and I'm flattered that they notice me.

Jody looks shocked every time she gets a comment, and the girl blushes a couple of times. I can tell that she doesn't want to be here. Jody doesn't have a curfew, but she goes home whenever I do, and I need to convince her to go somewhere in the first place. I don't understand her. If my parents would let me go where I please, I'd be out trying to have a little fun.

"Are my jeans too tight?" Jody asks.

"Of course," I reply. "Your jeans are supposed to be."

I don't know what she's worried about. My jeans are twice as tight as hers. Once you get used to them, they're not even all that uncomfortable. Jody's walking like it's an effort to move. She just needs to get used to wearing them. Suzy let her wear the jeans. Her mother understands about stuff like that.

I look around me. Things have picked up some, but not that much. A lot of guys are standing around near Burger King. Some look cute, but I don't go over there. I have doubts about some things. We head over near the Arcade instead. We were there earlier, and I beat my best score at Pinball.

At least Jody and I have done one "in" thing. We've been seen at Cassidy's. Everybody is always talking about the fun you can have here at night on the weekends, and it seems to be true. It would help if we were out later when things really start going, but I have a 10:30 curfew. I can't help that, but I'm going to have all the fun I can before my time is up.

"We're going to have some fun tonight!"

"Yeah, we're really going to party in an hour," Jody says in a down voice.

“Come off it, Jody,” I say. “We came here to party.”

“You came here to party,” she corrects me. “I'm here to keep you company.”

“You'll never get popular if you stay in the house all the time.”

“Big deal.”

“It is a big deal. You don't want to be a “straight” for the next four years.”

“What does it matter if we don't run around all the time? That doesn't make us “straights.” That’s such a stupid label.”

“Tell that to the guys.”

“I'm not going to be an airhead.”

“Who said anything about being an airhead?”

“I know you're thinking about Gale.”

“It wouldn't hurt us anyway if we were more like Gale.”

“Who gives a damn about Gale?”

“You're defeating the cause.”

“Who cares about the stupid cause?”

“I do. You know being popular is the only thing that I care about.”

Jody acts like she's ticked off. I only told her the truth. Being accepted means everything to me. I don't want to go around for the next four years while I'm at Central high school just stuck being a "nobody." There's nothing as relevant at school for me. I'm not too smart, and I'm not good at sports like Jody. Getting accepted is the only thing that could happen to me that would make me feel like I'm somebody special.

Sometimes it's hard to convince myself that I can be somebody exceptional. At home, it's like nobody wants to be bothered with me, and I spend most of my time feeling like I'm not even wanted. At school, it's like I'm on speaking terms with a lot of regular girls like me, and I'm always flirting with some average guy, but I want to be noticed by the top kids at school. I don't just fade into the background, but I'm not on center stage either. I know I'm pretty enough with my blond hair cut in its unique style by Jody after school last Monday, I have such a good personality, and I'm lots of fun to be around. I know Jody thinks us being too nice is the problem. Still, I see how Sheila Haskle is always acting friendly towards everyone, and it's like she's the most popular girl at school. I don't know if that's the main reason we're left on the sidelines. I worry that the people I want to impress will always think we're such "straights," and they'll never let us hang out with them, but at least we've done one cool thing – hang out at Cassidy's, so it should improve things for us some.

I see Mark leaning against a pole near Lib's Cookies. He's all alone. I'm glad to see him. He hasn't been in the vicinity of the school in a week, and I would have called him, but I didn't want to get anything started. His girlfriend thinks I'm trying to steal him away. Mark doesn't care, but I don't want any trouble with Linda Thomas. I'm not scared of her, but what's the use of fighting over a guy who's only a friend?

People are always going back and telling Linda shit. Mark and I are in three of the same classes, and we eat lunch together. Since we're friends, we sit next to each other during those classes we share, and there are a lot of jokes between us. Once, I gave Mark the answer to a Math problem. Somebody went back and told Linda that I was giving him my phone number. She never comes up to me about any of her suspicions. She takes it out on Mark. Causing them to fight and acting like she expects him to just drop our friendship. It seems like she's too scared to even talk to me about it. Still, since Jody is my best friend, and she's in her English class, she has been giving her the business and making her life miserable. Linda is a sophomore, she's on the Honey Bear squad, and she's so popular, so everybody treats her like she's "Ms. It" around the school, but she's not all that.

I could ease Linda's doubts about my relationship with Mark and assure her that we're only friends, but what do I care about what she thinks? If she wants to believe that I'm trying to steal her boyfriend away, then let her. Mark is free to talk to me if he wants to, and he's obviously willing to put up with all her shit to keep being around me. Going steady doesn't mean you own a person. Mark walks to school with Jody and me sometimes, and Linda acts like I'm putting the moves on him in that short amount of time. She talks about me behind my back, and she's always giving me those shitty looks of hers. Until she comes into my face with some shit, I'm not going to worry about it.

"Hey, Davis!" I call. "Come here!"

Mark walks towards us. He's cute, and he knows it, but he's not arrogant about it. Since he's been on the varsity football team, he's been getting a lot of attention from girls, and Mark could get a lot of dates just by being a jock. That's why I can't see why he stays with Linda. He's told me a lot of stuff about what they do, but I still wouldn't go steady with someone because of sex. There are too many willing girls around.

Mark has long blond hair and misty blue eyes. He's trying to grow a mustache, but it isn't getting anywhere. Mark has a couple of zits, but they're not that bad. He's about 6"1, and he has big feet. Mark's never out of tight jeans and t-shirts. When it was warmer, he just wore a t-shirt. Now that it's gotten colder, Mark's always wearing a plaid flannel shirt too. Mark's a freshman like Jody and me, but he's already sixteen, and he was driving for a while, but his car broke down. I guess that's when the trouble really started between him and Linda because she doesn't like to walk, and it's going to be a while before Mark can afford to fix his car.

Bitches like her just want things their own way,

and it takes most of your time just trying to please them. Linda should know that's why he runs to me more because we have a laid back relationship. Sometimes having somebody who understands him means more to a guy than you looking good by his side and acting like you're a prima donna that he owes everything to. Mark looks so good, and he's so decent, so I know he deserves a lot better than Linda.

"Hi, Moore," Mark says when he finally makes it over to where we're standing. "Hi, Travis. What are the two of you doing?"

"Nothing much," I say. "Did you play in the game?"

"Sure thing, I saw you and Jody there, but you weren't too interested in the game. Poor Eddie never had a chance."

"Mark! I was just talking."

"Oh sure, you're always chasing after guys," he teases me.

Mark smiles, and I smile back.

"Where's Linda?" Jody asks.

Good question. Linda never lets him out of her sight. She's afraid some girl will come along, and she will steal Mark away. Linda has a reason for her fears. Mark is gorgeous. I just love the way his eyes change color in various light, he has the perfect smile, and he is built terrific. I know we would be good together and whether I like it or not, I think about it. Sometimes,

I fantasize about us going out on a date and kissing all night long. Mark is really the only guy I have ever trusted. He's the only one I've ever had sexual dreams about, but that confuses me, and I can't understand why my mind would have that happen over a guy that I just want for a friend. The thing is, sometimes, I can only be around Mark, and my mind drifts off on romantic thoughts. I always stop myself when I start thinking that way because I know what the kids at school say is a lie. I didn't get close to Mark to steal him away.

"She doesn't know I'm here," Mark admits.

"Yeah, she'll want to hold your hand," I tease him.

I laugh, and Mark laughs back, but he wasn't laughing last month. Mark is this big, tough football player, and he's supposed to be able to take some pain, but Linda saw him get tackled by four guys during a game, and she ran out onto the field. Boy, was he embarrassed! Linda was noticeable in her Honey Bear uniform and pompoms. She was holding his hand and even crying. Mark wasn't hurt that bad, and he could have shaken the whole thing off after the Trainers got through with him, but I guess Linda just wanted to perform and get more attention than kicking up her legs got. Linda was down on the sidelines for the rest of the game, and she kept fussing over him. The guys gave it to him good when he got in the locker room, and I got an earful the next day. Sometimes, I just can't see why he puts up with that stupid bitch, because she is so dizzy.

"Don't knock it," Mark says. "It gets me a lot of tender loving care."

"That must be why you put up with her," I say.

We start joking around. Even Jody comes out of her shell when Mark's around. He has a way of doing that to you. Mark has a great sense of humor, and he keeps you laughing so much that you don't even have time to think about yourself. Sometimes, Mark can get silly, but he's a lot of fun. He's one of the reasons why I'm failing Math. We spend so much time in class fooling around that we don't get any work done.

"Way to go, Davis!"

There's this guy in this red Mustang yelling at Mark. I've seen him around the school, and he always acted like he owns the place or something. He runs around with Sheila Haskle and her crowd. He would never give anybody like Jody and me a glance, but tonight he acts like he's so drunk that anybody is all right for him to talk to.

Mark goes over to talk to the guy, and I walk across the parking lot over to Ridley Theatre. I look over the posters, but there's not an engaging movie I want to see. There's a good song on the guy's radio, and I start dancing. I can't help it. Whenever I hear music, it's like I've got to move. Sometimes, I even hear a beat in my head. I used to want to be a dancer when I was little, but my father was too cheap to let me take lessons at Mademe Trudy's School of Dance.

"Do you think my jeans make me look sexy?" Jody suddenly wants to know. I open my eyes, and I stop dancing. I look at the way Jody is standing like she's at attention. I tell her to let me see her walk. She's not walking like she's trying to look sexy.

"You're walking too stiff," I say.

"Thanks, thanks a lot. You're always telling me I need more confidence in myself, and then you tell me I walk too stiff."

I was only being honest, but I know Jody is hurt. I bet she's sorry that she broke the silence that has been between the two of us. While we were joking around with Mark, she didn't say two words directly to me. I don't want to get her mad again.

"Oh, Jody, you're super sensitive."

"I can never tell when you're lying."

"I'm not lying about this. You know I want you to have more confidence in yourself. You'll never get to be popular if you don't."

"You act like it's so easy."

"It is. You have to relax."

"It's hard to relax in these jeans."

"Hey, do you want to go for a ride?" the guy asks.

"Thanks, but no thanks."

I start walking off. Mark is in the car with the

guy, and it's apparent that they're going somewhere. I know when to get lost, but Jody heads towards the car. She hates the comments because they embarrass her. She doesn't like how the guys look at her, because she thinks it's degrading. She didn't even want to come to Cassidy's tonight, and she's been acting like she's doing me this big favor by sticking it out this long. But she's willing to hop into the first car that stops.

"Come on, Angel. This is your last chance. We can really party," Mark says.

"You can party without us tonight," I say. "Give us a rain check."

"Are you sure?" the guy asks.

He's been following along beside us. It's nice being noticed and all, but I wish he'd knock it off. Maybe it would be fun to go riding with them and get drunk, but I know word would get back to Linda before we had even left the parking lot. Besides, Mark isn't such a decent guy that he wouldn't want something for the ride. And the way the guy keeps looking at Jody, he's got the same thing on his mind. I'm not going to let things get out of hand and end up being an easy score. I know I'll have to handle it. Jody is biting her lip and waiting for me to answer.

"Positive!"

Jody blinks, Mark starts laughing, and the guy takes an I-don't-care-you're-the-one-who's-going-to-miss-out-on-the-fun-and-I'm-not-going-to-worry-about-it attitude, and there's a screech of tires. Mark is still yelling something as the car roars down the parking lot. I wait to hear it from Jody. She has to say something. Tell me I'm a bitch for getting shitty with the guy. She just has to say something.

"Do you know Mitch?" she asks.

"No. Do you?"

"Not really. We met at Roller World."

"You could have told me."

"There was nothing to tell. Mitch knocked me down. To prove he was sorry, Mitch brought me a Coke."

I'm dying of curiosity, but I decide to be mean. I want to know all the details. Like how Jody knows Mitch's name. I get around more than she does, and I didn't. Besides, what all happened at Roller World while she was roller skating? Jody looks down, and I feel guilty. I know she really wants to talk about the guy. Sometimes, I can hurt her without meaning to. When I want to do it – watch out.

"Oh, Jody, I'm sorry," I apologize to her.

"It's okay."

"What do you know about this, Mitch?" I ask. "Is he going steady with anyone?"

"Not that I know of," she says. "But that doesn't mean I have a chance with Mitch O'Connors."

"Why not? You're a good friend, and you're lots of fun to be around."

Jody is down on herself, and I try to make her feel better. She's always acting like she's not good enough for the kids at school. She's the most beautiful girl there, but she doesn't think she's that pretty. I don't know what's wrong with her. I think about the stuff she was saying earlier, and I think that has a lot to do with her lack of confidence. She can't change being mixed, so she might as well stop worrying about it. I don't really see what the big deal is. Not everybody is so small-minded by 1988, and it shouldn't even matter how she's made, because it doesn't change what kind of person she is. Maybe she just likes being miserable.

I catch sight of Ricky Flecher just ten feet away, and I stop in my tracks. I nudge Jody, and I lead her in that direction. I try to concentrate on something far ahead, so I won't look at him. It is so hard. We finally make it, and I try to stop my heart from beating so fast. I was late getting to school this morning, and I didn't get to follow my usual routine of walking down the hall where he stands at and trying to stand out from all the other girls doing the same thing. So it's really thrilling to have the chance to walk by without being surrounded by a crowd of girls and just blending in.

"Hey, baby! Wait up!"

We stop. Ricky had been sitting onto a car with

another guy. He has on mirror shades, and he was pretending not to watch the pretty girls who walked past. I'm glad Ricky noticed me. He must think I'm compelling if he decided to stop us.

I try to get my act together. I don't want to blow things. I finally have my chance to impress him, and I know I need to play it cool because if he decides I'm not hip, I'm not going to get a second chance to prove him wrong.

Ricky comes over to where we're standing. He has on this brown cowboy hat, and between that and the glasses, it's hard to make out his face. That's okay because I can recognize him. Anybody would. He's the most popular boy at school, and he's the best looking. The problem is, he knows it, and he's a little cocky, so I know he's the one in control, and I'm the one who needs to worry about how things go down.

"What's your name?" he asks.

"I'm Angel, and my friend's name is Jody."

"Angel, huh?"

"Yeah, but don't let the name fool you, because I don't deserve a halo."

"I haven't seen you around," he says. "You go to Central, don't you?"

"Yeah, and I've been around a lot," I admit. "You just haven't noticed."

"If you were around, I'd notice."

I get thrown off balance. What a compliment, especially coming from a guy like Ricky Flecher. I start blushing, and he smiles. I feel self-conscious around him. I guess it's because he's older and so important. I've wanted to meet him for so long, and I never thought I had a chance. So now that it's really happening, it's like being suspended in midair. Then, not knowing if there's a safety net beneath you. I decide to play it cool. I'm terrified, but he doesn't have to know that.

"What have you been up to?"

"Same things as everyone else, I suppose. Hanging out, having fun, staying stoned, and getting laid."

Jody looks like she feels like killing me. She's embarrassed, and besides, she knows I'm a virgin and that I never do anything except stay in the house. Well, he doesn't have to know I'm a "straight." Ricky wouldn't date anybody boring. The crowd he hangs around with is fast, and they do wild things. His group is the most "in" group at Central, and everybody knows how ultra-cool they are and how they like to party all the time. It's better to make him think I'm hip too.

"I guess I've got myself a hot one."

"I guess you do."

"Who are you getting it on with?"

"Nobody at the moment," I say. "I'm between conquests."

"How would you like me to be your next conquest?"

"If that's a line, I'm not biting."

"Your friend doesn't talk much."

"I know."

Jody gives us both dirty looks. It's not my fault that she isn't talking. She should be trying to make an effort to seem compelling to the guys. Ricky's friend isn't all that bad looking. At least I did try to go along with that Mitch O'Connors business. Jody looks like she's bored. I know she's never liked Ricky for some strange reason, but at least she doesn't have to act like she can't wait for the conversation to end.

"What's your name?" I ask, anyway.

"Ricky. Ricky Flecher and the guy back there puking is Johnny Roberts. He had a little too much to drink."

"Well, we all can't handle it."

"Yeah, I know what you mean."

"Do you know what time it is - uh, Ricky?"

"Yeah." He glances down at his watch. "It's only 11:45."

Oh no! I know I'm in for it now, and my curfew is all I can think about, but I don't want Ricky to see that I'm worried. I don't want all that work to be for nothing. I've tried too hard to make a good impression.

"Well, I guess I'll see you around."

Jody knows how worried I am about my stupid curfew. We start towards the payphone in a hurry. I know Dad is going to yell his head off about me being out so late, and he'll probably cause a scene in front of Jody. It's his fault anyway. It's stupid for someone my age to have a 10:30 curfew. What can you do in that short amount of time?

Jody starts giggling. I don't know what's wrong with her. She's never acted that way before. She's holding her stomach, and she keeps bubbling over. It's embarrassing. I wonder what's wrong with her, so I stop walking.

"What's the matter, Jody?" I ask.

"I'm Angel, but don't let the name fool you, because I don't deserve a halo."

Jody laughs.

Giggling is not enough. Jody had the nerve to laugh. If she thinks I was that bad, what must Ricky think? I start feeling silly. I tried so hard to impress him, and I must have made a big fool out of myself instead. That's the last thing I wanted to do. It would have been better for him not to have even noticed me at all.

"I'm sorry, Angel."

"Was I really that bad?"

"You were just super cool," she says. "I wish I

could be that calm when I'm talking to a guy."

"Are you sure? He's probably back there laughing his head off."

"If anything, he's wondering what hit him."

"Was I that good?"

"You know you were," she assures me. "I just wish you weren't so suggestive."

"What do you mean?"

"You know what I mean. I thought you were going to suggest Ricky take you riding. If you catch my drift."

"Jody! I was just teasing him. It is so embarrassing being a virgin."

"If you think hopping into bed with a jerk like Ricky Flecher is better, go right ahead."

"I will if I get the slightest chance."

"I believe you would. I think you'd actually have sex with an egotistical, self-loving jerk like Ricky just to get popular."

"Being popular has nothing to do with it," I say. "Ricky's wonderful."

"Sure, he's Mr. Wonderful," she says. "Until after he gets what he wants. You know the type."

"If I didn't know any better, I'd think you were jealous because Ricky focused all his attention on me."

"I was bored the whole time," she says. "I just think Ricky is a jerk."

"Will you quit saying that?" I ask. "If you can't say anything good, then don't say anything at all."

"Then I won't say anything."

"Suit yourself then," I say. "I'm going to call my dad."

I go over to the payphone, and I call Dad. I'm so upset about my fight with Jody that Dad going on and on about me being out so late doesn't even faze me, and I'm able to tune him out. It's just not fair. Jody is always talking about my attitude. She's always putting herself on a pedestal when she's comparing herself to me and talking about my bad faults, but she should start looking at herself. Just because I finally got Ricky to notice me and I teased him along, isn't any reason to get mad. Especially if she's supposed to be my best friend and she knows me better than everybody else. Ricky knew I was teasing him. It's nothing to get all upset about. But if that's the way she wants it, she can suit herself. I'm not going to apologize; once a night is enough. Besides, I'm not wrong.

CHAPTER 7

I woke up early this morning. I had trouble sleeping last night. I kept thinking about Jody. I know it's her fault that we had a fight, but I know I had some part in it too. It's not like I really have a chance with Ricky Flecher, and he does have an ego problem. Still, last night I wasn't thinking realistically, and that comment about him being an egotistical, self-loving jerk really hurt me.

We were supposed to go shopping today at Northland Mall. I get my allowance from Dad anyway, and after going through that hassle, I feel like going to the Mall just to make myself feel better. Dad can get so uptight just because he's giving me a lousy ten dollars, and he makes me feel like I should be guilty just because I'm even asking him for it. My father is just really cheap, and he can afford to get me a lot of appropriate things. Still, he acts like he hates doing anything for me at all. I go around looking worse than kids on Welfare because I've seen kids on free lunch who appear like a walking Fashion Show in all the latest styles. I'm dressed like a Goodwill reject most of the time.

I call Gale, but her mother doesn't know where she is. She has all the freedom she ever wants, and her parents never keep a close watch on her. Mark is out, because I don't want to piss Linda off. And I don't want to go by myself. I'm the type of person who needs somebody to talk to. I'm not enough company by myself, and I hate to be alone.

The phone rings and I go into my parents' room to answer it.

"Hello."

"Hi, it's me."

I don't say anything.

"You're not still mad, are you?"

I still won't answer.

"All right - I'm sorry I called Ricky a jerk."

"You didn't just call him a jerk," I remind her. "You called him an egotistical, self-loving jerk."

"That's why I said, I'm sorry. Do you still want to go to the Mall?"

"As long as you don't say anything about Ricky."

"Okay. Do you want me to come over there, or you come over here?"

"You come over here."

I hang up.

I knew she would apologize. Somebody had to, and I knew it wasn't going to be me. I'm glad everything is okay. I don't act like it most of the time, but I really like having Jody as a friend. She's the closest person I've ever gotten to. Mark is a good friend, but I don't tell him that much. I don't tell anybody everything about me. It's like I need to keep things to myself. I don't trust people not to laugh at me or think I'm stupid. I guess I don't think I have good ideas. I feel like everybody else's opinions are more acceptable, and they know what they're talking about. I never talk about what I'm really feeling. Mostly, I laugh and joke around a lot. It's easier to clown around than open yourself up and get rejected.

I go downstairs.

Jody is standing in the hallway. I give my father a dirty look. He could have asked her to sit down, but he's glued to the TV watching a football game. Nothing else is as important as far as he's concerned. At least my mother isn't around acting stupid. It's really embarrassing having parents like mine when Jody's parents made me feel so comfortable and at ease.

"Have a seat," I say. "We have a while before the bus comes."

"Thanks."

"I would invite you upstairs, but I'm not lucky enough to have a room as good as yours."

The TV is up loud, and Dad keeps giving us dirty looks, but we try to hold a conversation. Jody doesn't seem to mind about the way Dad is acting, but I get really ticked off. You would think as old as he is that he would know how to treat somebody's company. I'm glad when it's time for the bus.

I let Jody go out of the door ahead of me, and I make sure I slam the door as hard as I can. I hope the video goes out during an essential play. I take out a cigarette, and I light up. My parents don't like me smoking, but they don't give me a hassle about it. I guess it's because I could be out doing drugs, and it's better than that. Mom even cops them for me, and she doesn't complain that she needs to do that.

At the bus stop, there's this old lady. She acts like we're about to snatch her purse or something. She looks at us suspiciously, and she holds her handbag tighter. I guess she finally decides we are alright, and we're not going to hurt her because she starts talking to us.

"You remind me of my eldest daughter's girl, Cindy," she says. "Do you know Cindy Dickens?"

She's talking to Jody.

"No, I don't know her," Jody says. "Does she go to Central?"

"No. Cindy doesn't go to Central High School. She goes to Washington Middle School. She's smart but not as smart as her brother. Do you know Todd Dickens?"

"I'm a freshman. I don't know that many people."

"My Todd is a junior. His mother said he's about to..."

"Here's the bus," I interrupt them. Jody probably would have kept talking to the lady. She never knows when to give up. I don't have patience, and I never want to be bothered. Who cares about the lady's family? Seem like she would have something better to do than tell her family history to a couple of strangers.

On the bus, we head towards the back, and Jody sits by the window. The lady is upfront, and she starts talking to the man beside her. I turn my attention to Jody. She's looking out the window, and she seems deep in thought.

"How much money do you have?"

"Fifty dollars andthree of Suzy's credit cards."

"Boy, are you lucky. I had to beg to even get ten bucks, and you get fifty bucks and some credit cards without any problem at all."

"It's not so bad. I'll lend you some money if you really need it."

"Thanks. I wanted to put some jeans in the lay-a-way."

"Not another pair of Designer Jeans, I hope."

"What's wrong with Designer Jeans?"

"Nothing, if you just care about a label. I'll stick with my Levis."

"They're Name Brands jeans."

"I meant a pair of costly Name Brands jeans," she says. "My jeans cost under thirty dollars."

"These jeans only cost $75," I say. "It's not like I'm wearing a pair of $200 jeans like I see a lot of those rich girls at school in."

"You're paying all that money just for some Designer's name."

"It's just important to have clothes that say you have a sense of style. It's not like I'm trying to bankrupt my father by demanding he buy me some of those expensive jeans, but he's so cheap that he complained about the jeans I do have. Those Preps spend more money on jeans than I get spent on me in a year, so he should be happy that I only want some affordable jeans that cost under a hundred dollars."

"I guess it's hard. I've just never cared about paying more money just to wear some Designer's name on my clothes. My parents would pay for all that - it's just me."

"Why do you always try to be so different? Sometimes you have to do things to fit in with the other kids - not try to be an oddball."

"You sound like Gale."

"If that's a compliment, I'll accept it."

I guess Jody is pissed off, and she looks out the window again. I can't understand her. We go to a school like Central, where there are so many rich kids. There are all kinds of pressures to fit in. Most of the time, a person feels like an outsider anyway. It doesn't hurt to do a simple thing like try to dress like everybody else. It's like everybody wants to have Designer clothes and they cost a lot of money. Yes, the Preps have unlimited spending money to spend on expensive Designer clothes. They only compete among themselves, because none of the rest of us can afford to keep up with them. That's why we just buy affordable Designer clothes, and it's essential to have that label on your clothes.

I only have one pair of designer jeans, but I think it says something about me when people see that label onto my back pocket. I just want to belong at Central, and I feel like such an outsider anyway. Still, I really feel like I'm not "in" as far as clothes are concerned because my cheap-ass father hardly ever gives me any money for clothes. Still, if I'm fortunate, I can sneak and put something in the lay-a-way. That way, he needs to buy me what I want, but I can't do that too often, so I'm left out on having all the decent clothes I want.

I think having Designer clothes is such a big deal at Central and nobody wants to feel left out. Yes, some losers come to school wearing clothes that look like they came from some Discount Outlet Store, which has their clothes looking irregular. Mostly everyone dresses decent, though. Even all those poor kids who get bused from the southside of town all come to school looking like they have the latest Designer fashions on. A lot of the time, I'm miserable because I can't keep up with the Preps. Still, I tell myself, at least I'm not looking like one of those losers who look like they can't afford any decent clothes at all. Even if sometimes I feel like my clothes do say I've picked something out of a rejected Goodwill pile, I don't look as pitiful as those kids. I know I just stay resentful because I can't get my dad to put out any significant money for clothes for me, and I get jealous of how the Preps have things. For once, I want to be able to go into the bathroom and be able to brag about how much something I'm wearing costs and act mad that I didn't get to spend even more money. I know I'm dreaming, though, because my dad will never stop being such a cheap-ass, and I'll always have to be stuck with the stupid clothes I do have. I'm even lucky that I do have at least one pair of designer jeans.

Jody is so lucky that she has so much money and she can afford to buy all the Designer clothes she wants, so I don't know why Jody acts like she can't do that. Kids just dress a certain way, and it's like our identity. That's why I can't understand why Jody wants to be so different. It's like she's always doing something to prove that she's not trying to fit in at school. I feel like Jody could really have a chance at popularity if the girl put some effort into it. Instead, she resists my every attempt to make things better for us. I'm tired of being a "straight," and I hate getting left out of everything. I want to be accepted and so well-known that lots of kids are always calling me up and wanting me to go out with them to do some exciting things. Sometimes, I think about how it's going to be, and I know things will be so much better than they are now. I really like being Jody's friend, and we have a lot of fun together, but I want other friends too because I just want a lot of kids to hang out with.

I know I am only a freshman, and I'm not expected to just take over at school, but I want my chance to prove that I can be somebody special at Central. I think about being a top girl and having all the kids think I'm somebody important. I get tired of just floating along at Central, never feeling like I'm a part of anything. It's like everyone thinks Jody and I are such "straights," and they never invite us to do anything with them. I want to go to cool parties and hang out with the popular kids and just feel like I belong. I want some top guys like Ricky Flecher and Tony Phillips to be interested in me, and I want to date some guys like that. Sometimes, I feel like such an outsider at school, and I just want to be "in" for once.

Sometimes, it's like things are just a certain way at Central. I know somebody like me doesn't stand a chance, and I will get shunned forever if I don't do what it takes to change my situation. I feel like I want to fit in more and have all the kids like me. I see the kind of respect that girls like Sheila Haskle and Cathy Rankin get, and I want to have that kind of attention myself. I feel like I'm always watching the popular girls at school and feeling so jealous of them because they have things so great. I know I only resent the Preps so much because I want to be just like them. Rich kids rule at school, and I can't do anything about the money situation, but I want to break into one of their cliques anyway.

I know when I'm accepted, I will have things made. I will never have to worry about everybody liking me. I will have more confidence in myself because I will know I'm not such a loser. Sometimes, I don't like myself very much, and I think negatively about myself. I feel so unimportant sometimes, and I never feel like I'm special. I get totally ignored at home, so I want to have school mean so much to me. I think about having all the kids like me and those kids going out of their way to show me how special they think I am. Is that too much to ask for?

Jody won't talk to me, so I look towards the front. This good-looking guy is sitting on the first seat. I see him looking in the mirror. I catch his glance, and then I look away. I play a game of cat and mouse with him. I look in the mirror, and he's staring back at me. I do it a couple more times. The next time I look in the mirror, he's smiling at me. I smile too, shyly. The man in the seat ahead of ours gets up, and he blocks my view. He gets off the bus, and the guy takes his place. He turns around in the seat, and he grins. I give him a dazzling smile, and I'm full of confidence because I know I caught him in my trap, and it just proves that I've still got it.

“Can I go where you're going?” he asks.

It's not the best pick-up line, but I don't care about brains.

“Let me think about it.”

The guy has blond curls and blue eyes. His cheekbones aren't that bad either. His lips are just a little pouty, and I can see myself kissing them. There's really nothing wrong with him, and I know he’s a good catch. It would be fun having him along for our shopping trip. It’s no big secret, but I like just about every guy I see. Unless he's ugly and he has zero personality. This guy doesn't have to worry about any of that. He's hot, so I'm glad to have him interested in me. I know I should just tease him along and play hard to get, but I really like him, and I can see us dating sometimes.

"Well?" he asks.

“Sure, why not?”

”What are your names?”

“I'm Angel Moore, and my friend's name is Jody Travis.”

“Glad to meet you,” he says. “I’m Russ Jones.”

“Do you go to Central?”

“Yeah, I'm a freshman.”

"Oh."

He would be a lousy freshman. I don't want to get involved with someone like that. I want an older guy. Preferably Ricky Flecher, but I'm not going to think about him. I need to think about getting rid of Russ Jones.

"You sound disappointed," he says.

"I'm not. I just thought you were older."

"Lots of people think that."

Jody finally comes alive, and she starts looking at Russ. She has this big smile on her face, and she acts like she's checking him out. I'm surprised. She's never interested in guys. She always says I talk about them too much, and she forever acts like she's bored with the whole subject.

"I like your smile," Russ tells her.

"That makes us even," Jody replies. "Because I like your grin."

I stare at her in a state of shock. Did Jody said that? Shy Jody Travis. The girl who blushed last night when some guy said he liked her tits. I can't believe it. Maybe she's coming out of her shell. I look at Russ. Perhaps he did it. I need to pull the buzzer. If I had left it up to Jody, we would have missed our stop. Russ tags along after us when we get off the bus at Northland Mall. Jody keeps smiling. Maybe she remembers what Russ told her. They end up holding hands. I just look at the two of them.

"What do you want to do first?" Russ asks.

"Go to the Jeans Shoppe," I say. "You sure you won't find shopping boring?"

"I'm sure."

"Yeah, we'll have fun," Jody says.

At the Jeans Shoppe, I look for jeans, and Jody hangs out with Russ. She hasn't let go of his hand once. Russ keeps telling jokes, and Jody keeps laughing. I don't know why, but it bothers me. Maybe it's ego. Russ was interested in me, but now he's acting like Jody is so exceptional. I go into the dressing room, and I leave the two of them alone.

I try on my jeans. Two pairs of jeans are too small. I like tight jeans, but I know I'll never pull off wearing jeans that tight. I take the jeans I want, and I go back over to where Jody and Russ are standing. Jody tries to act innocent, but she should know lipstick shows up good on a guy. I can't believe her. Last night she was acting silly over Mitch O'Connors and today she's kissing a guy she's hardly known an hour. And she has the nerve to talk about the way I behave around guys!

"Russ, you're crazy," Jody gushes.

"Yeah, really hilarious," I say. "Aren't you getting anything?"

"Not here. Maybe later," Jody says. "Russ invited

us to go for Cokes."

"Let me put my jeans in the lay-a-way first."

I go over to the counter, and I wait to pay the deposit on my jeans. There's a long line. I'm glad when I finally get through. We start walking towards The Shack. Jody and Russ keep up their conversation. It's apparent that they want to be alone, but Jody would never tell me that. I bet Russ wishes I would get lost. It makes me feel like a fifth wheel or something.

"I wonder why we've never met around the school," Russ says.

"I don't know. We're freshmen too."

I give her a dirty look. Great Jody. Tell him we haven't had dates this year either.

"Whose homerooms are you in?" Russ asks.

"I'm in Rogers. Angel is in Douglas."

"I'm in Thomas's homeroom. He's a rat."

"I've heard that. Is Mr. Thomas really that bad?" Jody asks like she really wants to know.

"Well, he is tough."

The Shack isn't that big. Booths are lining one wall, and we take stools around the counter. Russ orders the Cokes, and I swirl around on my seat. They talk, but I don't have anything to say. It's boring. Jody is hanging onto Russ's every word and looking impressed. If I didn't know Jody any better, I'd think it was a big act. She's trying too hard. You should keep a guy guessing. Not show him how much you like him.

"Do you pick up girls a lot?" I finally ask.

"Nah, why do you ask?" Russ wants to know.

"Because you're so good at it, and I was wondering if it was a hobby or something."

"I was coming here anyway. I heard Jody talking about coming here too, so I thought we'd hang out together. I'm leaving after the Cokes anyway."

"You don't have to do that. Does Russ, Angel?"

"I wasn't suggesting anything."

"I really have to go." Russ stands up. "I'll see you around, Jody. Bye Angel."

Russ leaves, and Jody won't look at me. About ten minutes pass. I didn't do anything to drive him away, but I don't think Jody agrees. I guess she was really hung up on the guy. Jody doesn't have any experience at all. It would be like her to fall for a guy just like that. I wasn't trying to cause any problems for her, but the guy isn't worth it. Look how fast he flipped from me to her when I lost interest in him. He wasn't that great, to begin with, and he would have only ended up hurting her feelings, so I really did her a big favor if you ask me.

"You didn't have to do that," she finally says.

"I didn't tell him to leave."

"You didn't have to. You kept looking at your watch and sighing. Even I got your message."

"He's just a freshman," I remind her. "You don't need a freshman."

"What has age got to do with it?"

"I just think you can do better," I say. "Anyway, what about Mitch O'Connors?"

"I just think Mitch is exciting," she admits. "I don't have a chance with him."

"How do you know?" I ask. "Besides, I know Mitch isn't a freshman. You see his nice car? Why do you want to walk with a freshman when you can be driving with an upperclassman? Boys our age are so immature, and they know nothing. That's why we need to get some older guys to date and have fun with. You can look like that all you want, but you know I am right."

"I give up."

"You ready to go shopping?" I ask.

"Yeah, just let me finish my Coke."

That stupid jerk went off without paying for our Cokes, so after I pay for my own Coke, I only have forty cents left. I hope Jody remembers her promise. I hate asking her for money, but she doesn't seem to mind. It's not like I'm just using her for some money because she's so affluent. I feel awful about being in the position where I even need to borrow twenty dollars to at least be able to buy me something cheap at the Mall. I feel like my father makes a decent amount of money as an Insurance Man, and we could live better, but he's so cheap, and he hates spending a dime on anything worthwhile. That's why we don't have cable or anything like that. I feel like Jody knows she's a true friend of mine, and I wouldn't use her for her money, and she's not always trying to buy my friendship like Gale is, but I still don't feel right about the whole thing, and I try to shake those feelings.

I can't wait until I'm old enough to work, and I can have my own money. Then I can quit depending on my stupid father for everything and having him do every little thing for me. Then always hearing his big mouth complaining about the measly stuff that he even does. Sometimes my pride can't take the begging, and I just do without. But it's embarrassing when you don't have any money, and you want to do things. Sometimes, I really hate being middle class and having my dad complain about all our bills. Knowing we'll never have enough money to live better. I really wish I could be rich like Jody and have my mother give me her credit cards and still give me fifty dollars on top of that. That will never happen. I'll be lucky to even get my ten dollars allowance out of my dad and be forced to hear his mouth just because he's given me that lousy amount of money. So what? Some things will never change.

CHAPTER 8

After a long day of shopping, it's good to get back to Jody's house. I went back, and I got my jeans out of the lay-a-way at the Jeans Shoppe, and Jody also lent me the money to buy a pair of boots at Boot Town and three tops at Ashley Nicole. I felt funny inside after borrowing the money because my jeans cost $95.00, my boots cost $75.00, and my tops came to $120. I should have just said "no," but Jody talked me into getting the boots, and she insisted on getting my jeans and tops too. I told her I'm going to pay her back, and I am. I don't care if it'll take a long time.

It just feels so good to finally have something fashionable to wear, because usually, I need to struggle to even get my better-than-nothing-at-all clothes. I get so embarrassed sometimes about the way I look, and I always wish I could dress better. The kids that matter go around in Designer clothes all the time, and it says something about them. I forever feel like a misfit, because the only Designer jeans I had were from last year and they are well worn, so everybody knew I couldn't keep up with the latest trends. The only way I can even get some halfway decent clothes is to put them in the lay-a-way and trick my cheap-ass father into buying me something new.

Jody goes back to talk to Tom in the backyard, and I go use the phone in the living room. So far, I've counted three phones. There's even a phone in Jody's bedroom. Jody said she has her own separate line and everything. I keep trying to stop comparing my life to hers and knowing how lucky she is, but it's so hard.

I dial home. "Hello."

"Dad, it's me, Angel."

"What do you want?"

I forgot. Saturday football games are on. Watching two teams play that dumb game is more important than talking to his daughter.

"Dad, can I spend the night?"

"You were out late last night," he reminds me. "Isn't that enough?"

"Jody really wants me to stay," I say. "We went shopping today."

"I hope you didn't put anything in the lay-a-way," he says. "You always do that."

"I didn't," I say. "Jody lent me some money."

"You know I don't like you to do that," he says. "That girl's parents will think I don't provide for you."

"They won't," I say. "Jody's parents are loaded, and they don't care about money."

"Well, I'm not loaded, and I have to care about money. I spend eight hours a day hustling and struggling to sell Goddamn Life Insurance Policies to people who don't even worry about dying. They treat me like shit because they don't want to plan for the inevitable the way they should. But are you grateful because I go through all that crap every day, so you'll have a roof over your head and food to eat? No, you're always complaining about something you want and acting like I'm made of money. Then throwing up in my face how much money your friends have and what their parents are willing to buy for them. You can spend the night with that girl all you like. Just don't come back here tomorrow, thinking you're going to be spending up a storm. We all can't afford it."

Click.

Dad doesn't wait to see if I have anything else to say. He just hangs up on me. If I had hung up during his speech, he would have gotten mad. But who am I, only his lousy daughter? I'm not worthwhile.

Jody comes back, and I tell her that I can spend the night. She breaks out in a big smile. I smile back. I'm glad to be getting out of the house too. Maybe I'm making progress with my parents. I've really gotten out a lot this weekend.

"Do you want to go to the store now?" Jody asks. "We can wait 'til later, but I thought you'd want to get it over with."

"We can go now."

Jody says that Simmons Market isn't too far away. We start talking about the kids at school. I think about how everyone is always saying I'm trying to steal Mark away from Linda. I know Jody feels that way too. I like him a lot, but I'm not sure if I like him that way.

"What do you think about Mark?" I ask.

"What do you mean, what do I think about Mark?"

"About our relationship. You know what everyone is saying, don't you?"

"Yeah, that you're trying to steal him away."

"Do you think that way too?"

"Kind of, I think you should go after him. Let's face it. Linda is a big dope, and you two would make a good couple."

"I don't see it that way."

"Admit it, Angel," she says. "You really like Mark."

I won't admit anything. Instead, I kick a can towards Jody. We kick it back and forth for about five blocks, and then we lose interest. I don't want Jody to know she's right. She can read me so well. I don't know if I like that or not.

"Okay, Jody, you win," I finally say. "I really do like Mark, but it doesn't change things."

"Why not? You two belong together."

"For one thing, he's going steady with Linda.

"He would dump her in a second if you gave him the okay."

"The other thing is, he's only a freshman."

"What's this thing you've got about age?"

"I don't know. Diane only dated older guys. I don't want to break the pattern."

"That's really it, isn't it?" she asks. "You're still trying to beat Diane out."

"I didn't say that."

"You didn't have to. I'm your best friend. You can't keep everything from me."

I don't say anything. Jody really hit a sore spot. If she can read me like that, I bet it won't be long before everyone else can too. Jody is my best friend, but I don't want her knowing everything about me. I want to be secretive. That way, people will wonder what I'm about.

Inside Simmons Market, I don't have to worry about it. Jody and I act like little kids. It's a small grocery store, and we go around getting a lot of stuff we don't need, and we fill up a shopping cart. When we get the things that we want, Jody throws them in the cart. When we are at the counter, Jody goes through her Mae West imitation, and I keep making faces.

The lady in front of us finally gets finished, and we move our shopping cart up. I almost die of embarrassment. The best looking guy I have ever seen is ringing up our stuff on the cash register. I just keep staring at him. He has dreamy blue eyes. His brown hair is in a crew-cut, but it doesn't look bad. His cheekbones are terrific too. His arms are muscular, and I bet the rest of him is really built also.

He picks up the sacks without any trouble, and he hands one to Jody and me. I keep looking back at him, and he winks. I think my heart is never going to stop beating so fast. I almost trip, and I finally turn around. Jody is already at the corner, and I need to walk in a hurry to catch up to her. Just thinking about the guy makes me sigh.

"Jody, did you get a look at that guy?"

"That's all you ever think about," she says. "Guys, guys, guys."

"Never mind that," I say. "Did you see that guy?"

"Who could miss him?"

"He's even better than Ricky."

"Forget what I said. Think about other guys, anything to get your mind off Ricky Fletcher."

"Ricky, who?"

"Now, you see why I come here all the time. You should see the place after school. Girls are swarming around everywhere."

"Is that where you are at every day?"

"Well, naturally."

"I wonder what his name is."

"Greg Tyler."

"Greg Tyler," I say softly.

"Take it easy, Angel. It's just a guy. I thought you were above getting this excited over a guy."

"I'm not above nothing," I assure her. "How do you know Greg's name anyway?"

"I asked him, of course."

"You asked him? You actually walked up to that good-looking guy, and you asked him his name?"

"What's the big deal about?"

"The big deal is that you go around pretending to be shy."

"I don't pretend anything. When I have something to say, I say it."

"I'll never doubt you again. If you can talk to a guy like that, you don't need any lessons in confidence. You pass the course with an A+."

“Let's quit the kidding around about guys 'til we get to my room,” she says. “I don't like that kind of talk around Tom. “

“Why not? He wouldn't get mad, would he?”

“Of course not,” she tells me. “Tom's not that strict. I just like to keep him thinking I'm Daddy's Little Girl.”

“You have a strange relationship with your parents.”

“We're just different.”

“I didn't mean anything offensive,” I tell her. “I think it's great.”

Anything is better than what I have with my parents. At least her parents give her attention, and she has a relationship with them. It's better than not getting bothered with at all.

CHAPTER 9

Today has been the closest Jody and I have ever been. We've been talking a lot, and she seems to have gotten a lot of stuff off her chest. Her parents really bother Jody. I mean them not being married bothers her. She has a lot of fears and things about them breaking up. Jody is even too scared to sleep away from home. She thinks they will just go off and leave her while she's away because Jody said when she was younger, Jody was separated from them for a while. Jody almost had a nervous breakdown or something, so I know it is something serious. I don't think it was anything that she ever did that caused her parents to leave her, but Jody has it in her head that she was disobedient then, so most of the time now, she acts goody-goody. I can see how much her parents love her, and I can't imagine them hurting her on purpose. I try to reassure her, but I don't know if it makes things any easier.

I've been talking too. I've shared so many things

with Jody. I've never been able to confide to anyone the way I can to Jody. Usually, I just talk about nonsense stuff that doesn't matter. It's hard opening yourself up and telling people what you really feel. I spend most of my time joking around, and I know nobody really takes me seriously except for Jody. I always think that nobody else would care about my opinions or believe that my ideas are any good. I know I'm not so smart, and I don't want people to think I'm a dummy. I feel like Jody respects my opinions, and she even seeks my advice, and that really makes me feel good because nobody has ever done that before. I'm glad we can be so close to each other. I like having somebody I can depend on. Even if I act so aggressive all the time, I've always wanted to have somebody to share things with and just be able to let down the guard around them. Jody is the best friend I've ever had, and she has always been there for me, and I hope I never do anything to blow our friendship because I never want this closeness to end.

The only other person I can talk to is Mark, but lately, my thoughts have been getting weird, and I really don't know how I feel about him. I've been trying to keep a certain distance towards him, and I don't try to get too comfortable with him. He tells me stuff about Linda, and I tell him about my bad luck with the guys. He listens, and I listen. We don't try to give each other any unwanted advice. I get along well with Mark. I've never been friends with a guy before, and my mind gets to wandering, and I am thinking about how it would be like to date him. It's been happening more and more lately, but I try to push it away because I don't want to think that way.

I decide to ask Jody about it.

"I've been thinking," I tell Jody.

"About what?"

"You know, before."

"We've talked about so many things."

"About Mark."

"What about him?"

"You know, I think I really like him," I admit. "I mean, the way I would like a boyfriend."

"Why don't you tell him?"

"Are you crazy?" I ask. "He'd think I'm kidding and do something like a laugh in my face."

"I doubt that," she says. "The way he looks at you, I bet he'd be glad."

"I don't know. It's hard to take that risk and be rejected."

"You never worry about that with other guys," she reminds me. "You're always coming on to them."

"It's because they don't matter to me. It's different when you think someone is special, and you're taking a chance."

"I guess so."

"Anyway, I haven't given up on Ricky Flecher."

"Remember what we agreed."

"Just because we talk about him doesn't mean we have to fight."

"Okay, as long as you don't get offended if I don't like him."

"I'm just looking out for myself. Mark can't do anything for me. Ricky can make all my dreams come true." I give her a look. "You're not really hung up on that Russ Jones, are you?"

"I really like him," she says. "I know I don't know Russ, but when I kissed him, it was special."

"Last night, you thought Mitch O'Connors was really special."

"I still do. I don't want to think about just one boy. I'm too young. I don't want to get serious until I'm at least a senior. Russ seems more attainable than Mitch."

"You have to strive for the best. If everybody just settled for anything, where would we be? That's why I'm going after Ricky Flecher. I have about one chance in a thousand, but I'm going for it. I already have him interested."

"Knowing you, I bet you'll do it."

"Yeah, and I'll be "in." I'll be accepted and hanging out with the 'in' group. There will be parties on top of parties, and I'm going to have all the fun I can. Everybody will look up to me. Even Diane will be impressed."

"That's what you really want, isn't it?" she asks. "It's for Diane to pay attention to you."

"Uh, well... I guess so."

"It must be hard."

"Diane's always treated me like I'm nothing. Even when we were little, and I wanted to talk, she'd tell me to shut up. When her friends come over, she makes me get out of the room, and most of the time, she acts like I don't even exist."

"You shouldn't let it get you down."

"I don't. Don't worry about me. Diane will never change, and I don't care. It would be different if she wasn't adopted. My parents go out of their way to make sure things are perfect for her, and she accepts it like it's her due."

"What a bitch."

"You're telling me. The thing that gets me is why come my parents can't see all the bad things she does. Like the weed. Diane is so stoned out of her head sometimes that she seems to be in another world. But they are so dumb. You can get anything past them. I've been drinking for over four years, and it seems like some morons would notice that, but they never say anything at all about it. It's like they hide their heads in the sand and act as if they don't acknowledge the problem, then it will just go away, and they won't have to deal with it. No wonder Diane and I are so fucked up. Dad will go on for fifty years over money or if I'm a second late for curfew, but he ignores the real problems which affect my life. They don't even care what I do and when I try to get their attention, they act like I'm bothering them."

"I didn't know it was so hard."

"I know the drinking is my fault, and I made the decision to start, but sometimes I think I can't even stop, and I get scared, and I want them to help me, but my pleas go on deaf ears. They are my parents, and they should know that I am going through something, and I shouldn't have to spell it out for them."

"I haven't said anything about your drinking, but that doesn't mean I don't care," she says. "Remember how sick I got when I sneaked out those beers for us to drink? I've never done anything like that before, but I didn't want you to think I was a big baby."

"I shouldn't always pressure you to do things," I say. "Your parents trust you so much, and you never felt like going behind their backs before. I feel like I'm corrupting you."

"You haven't forced me to do anything I didn't want to do," she says. "I've become tougher since I've been hanging around you. I know I can't hide under Tom and Suzy all the time, because they need some time alone too. I just could never depend on anybody else before, and I never felt confident enough to stand alone. Before I met you, I just had surface friends, and I wouldn't even bring them home to meet my parents. I never told them anything at all about me. I should be glad that we left New York because I was turning into a professional liar, and I felt awful all the time. I know having an interracial family isn't such a big deal in 1988, but it's harder when the father is white. People can accept a white woman with a black man, and they just figure she's trash anyway. And none of the white men even want her. But Tom is so damn good-looking and white women look at Suzy like she doesn't even deserve him. They hate her because she's taken one of their good men and not just somebody nobody wants anyway. Reverend Davis even said a lot of shit to her, and I guess he thinks that Heaven is going to be segregated because he thinks the races shouldn't mix."

"Carsonville is just like that," I tell her. "The blacks stay on the southside of town, and the whites live among the other parts of town. Not over six black families have crossed over that invisible line and mixed together. I'm even surprised that black kids get bused to Central now, but you see that they don't even try to talk to us and act like they're happy to just hang out together. Sometimes, I wonder why they are even at school because I thought the whole point of having them there was for us all to get along and just blend into one happy group."

"There's no school spirit anyway, and Central is the pits," she says. "Queen Cathy Rankin rules, and she feels like she has the right to dictate how everyone else should be. Cathy's infamous Slam List is still a sore point for everyone, and I think the bitch just knows she's not really shit, so she needs to keep putting other people down just to pretend she is. I don't care what the bitch thinks about me, but I could see that Cathy got to a lot of the other kids. Especially, the ones she didn't think rated enough to even make that Slam List. It's awful to be labeled, but worse not to be visible enough to get noticed in the first place. I think Cathy's the only fool who really even deserves to be treated the way Ricky Flecher dogs her out, and I wish that he would really break her down."

"I can't stand her either."

"I hate her with a passion," Jody says, but she doesn't explain why. "But I don't want to talk about that. We were talking about your parents, and we got off the subject."

"When I called Dad today to ask if I could stay the night, he acted like I was wasting his time. Like the football game that he was watching was more important than me. Then he hung up on me. He didn't wait to see if I had anything else to say. You're lucky to have a father the way he is."

"Tom likes football."

"But I bet he's not a nut about it. We can't watch anything else when Monday Night Football is on. He acts like there's nothing else important."

"Maybe you ought to talk to him when he's not

busy," Jody suggests.

"You don't know what it's like. Dad never has the time for me. He thinks I'm either after money or trying to pull something. Not that Dad's about to give me any money. He's so cheap that he hardly even wants to give me any money, so I always go to Mom. She'll give me five dollars without any hassle. And the only reason I'm always trying to pull stuff on him is that he never lets me do anything."

"Is that why you always have to call him?"

"Yeah, as soon as I get in the middle of having fun, then I have to call him. And he never wants me to do stuff in the first place. I need to beg and beg, and if I'm getting a break, I can go somewhere for a couple of hours. You're lucky you don't have a curfew."

"I have enough sense to come home."

"Like I don't. I may act like I'm irresponsible, but I'm a very responsible person. I know how to take care of myself. It's just that they never give me the chance to prove myself. If you were being put down all the time and talked to like you couldn't do anything right, you'd find it hard to go out of your way to show you can do stuff too."

"'Hmmm."

"We don't want to spend the whole night talking about me," I say. "Are you getting along with your parents now? I know how you said you had to talk to them about some problems you were having."

“Yeah, things are great between us again, and having that talk with them last Friday was better than going out with you and Gale. You said your parents wouldn't let you go anyway, and I would have been mad if I had been stuck with her for the whole night. I told Tom and Suzy about everything you and me had been up to, and I let them know how left out I'd been feeling, so everything should stay all right. Even my grandparents are finally coming around, and I don't hold a lot of old stuff against them anymore. We've even been over there for dinner, and they've pretty much accepted Tom. They don't welcome him like the Prodigal Son, but things are okay.”

“I know you were worried about that. See? That's the difference between you and me. Everything works out for you. My life will be a mess for years to come.”

“Don't say that,” she says. “You make me feel guilty.”

“What have you got to feel guilty about? It’s not your fault. I wish you could choose the people who are going to be your parents. I sure wouldn’t pick mine.”

“Things will work out.”

“Hmmm.”

I know it's a hopeless subject. Nothing will ever change with my parents. They'll always treat me like a Nobody and try to make my life as miserable as possible. Jody is lucky. Even if she didn't have this house and all her money, I'd still be so jealous of her. It's because of the great relationship Jody has with her parents. Jody gets upset because she gets left out of a few conversations, and she acts like her life is over. How would she feel if there was never any communication like in my family, and she never got treated exceptionally in the first place? Tom and Suzy would do anything for her. Thinking about that suddenly gives me a great idea. I'd probably have a hard time convincing Jody of it, but it might work out. It wouldn't hurt to ask her.

"Hey, I have a great idea."

"What?"

"You don't have a date for the Follies, do you?"

"You know I don't."

"Tom will do anything for you, won't he?"

"Sure, but what has that got to do with anything?"

"Let him take you to the Follies."

"Why would I want my father to take me to the Follies?"

"Nobody knows he's your father, and he'll make a great date for you. Look how young and gorgeous he is."

"That's crazy," she says. "Anyway, what's in it for you?"

"What do you mean?"

"You never just do anything for anybody, and you know it. Something needs to motivate you. That's why I want to know what you're going to get out of it."

"Thanks, Jody. Thanks a lot. I put myself out for you, and you put me down."

Something snaps in me. I start crying, and I can't stop. I keep thinking about Jody being the only person I trust and her having that kind of opinion of me. We're supposed to be best friends, and if she thinks that lowly of me, I'd hate to know what the other kids at school think. I won't look at Jody. In a way, I blame her for what's happening. I haven't cried since I was a little girl and I don't want to do it now. I feel like such a sissy, and I hate acting like such a little kid.

"I'm sorry, Angel," Jody says. "I didn't mean to make you cry."

"I'm not crying," I insist. "I've just got something in my eyes."

"It's okay to cry. Everybody does, even Tom."

"I don't. It means you're weak."

"No, it doesn't. I told you Tom cries when he's upset. You should never hide your emotions."

"You do," I tell her. "All the time."

"Well, not anymore, I won't. Like today, I talked to Russ. Usually, I stand around like a dope, and I wait for someone else to make the first move. Today I took a chance, and you see what happened. That's why I don't think it's a fear anymore. I may get laughed at yet, but I'm not going to stand around and wait for it not to happen."

I don't know what to say after that confident speech. Jody hasn't talked that tough since I've known her. I guess she's surprised too. She looks like it. I know it is okay to show your emotions sometimes. Especially when you're around somebody who's not going to laugh at you and make you feel so stupid. But I'm not going to change at school. If the kids thought I wasn't as strong as I pretend to be, they'd go out of their way to hurt me.

"What were we talking about before?" I ask.

"I don't know."

"Oh, yeah," I say. "The Follies."

"I was hoping you'd forget."

"If you don't want to do it, okay."

"That's the problem," she says. "I do."

"You do?"

"Yeah, but what if I go ahead, and everybody recognizes the resemblance between Tom and me?"

"They won't. Anyway, you don't look too much like Tom. You look mostly like Suzy, except the color, of course."

"Thanks. That's the nicest thing anybody has

ever said about me."

"You know, you're lucky in some ways. You can date anybody you want. I remember when I was in fifth grade, there was this black guy I liked a lot, but everybody thought I was crazy, so I pretended I was just kidding about it. You don't have that problem."

"It's not as easy as you think. I've never dated for that reason. I've gotten asked out a lot, but I always turned the guy down. I'm attracted to both races, but I'm confused. I know it would be hard either way I go."

"I never thought about it that way. I guess it could be awkward. Anyway, I heard Sheila Haskle talking about going out with Lenny Michaels. If she does that, it will be okay for anybody to date anybody. Everything Sheila does becomes the "in" thing to do. Before you know it, it will be chic to date a black guy, and all the white girls will want one just to fit in. I can see it now, all the cool white girls having token black boyfriends and all the white guys not being able to get a date anymore, so they turn to the black girls to give them a chance. Maybe everyone would finally start hanging around each other then, and everything would work itself out."

"It doesn't matter to me," she says. "I guess I'll stick with Russ."

"If my plan works, Mitch will notice you."

"Do you really think it'll work?"

"Sure, it will. Girls will be envious, and they'll be

talking. I bet even Mitch will hear about it, and he'll want to get to know you."

"I think you're expecting a lot, but I'm willing to try."

"Just wait until Thursday night. You'll have to give the performance of your life. I can't wait to see you."

"I'll try," Jody says. "That's the only thing I can do."

I didn't think Jody would go along with my plan, but she gets excited about it. We spend a long time talking about the whole thing, and it looks like everything is going to be okay. Mitch O'Connors is just about as influential as Ricky Flecher. If Jody started going out with him, she would be popular because she's his girl, and because I'm her best friend, people would notice me too. I wouldn't use Jody just to get accepted, but if it happened by accident, I wouldn't go out of my way to stop it.

CHAPTER 10

I don't know how the subject was brought up. We were just sitting on Jody's bed talking about boys, and then we started discussing sex. I guess she's been thinking about what I said about having sex with Ricky Flecher. I was just teasing him, but Jody thinks he took me seriously. And she's having doubts about letting Russ Jones kiss her so soon. Jody believes she should have gotten to know him better.

"A girl like Gale Stewart acts like it isn't such a big deal. She's only fourteen, and I bet she's had sex with just about every guy at school," Jody says.

"Gale's looking for love. You don't know how her parents are. They act like the money they give her is enough. I don't know if she's getting loved, but look at all the guys she has."

"Guys are just using her. Ed Redding said you just have to buy her a Big Mac and a Shake, and she's willing to put out."

"I heard something like that too."

"I don't like Gale, but I feel sorry for any girl who puts herself down like that. She acts like she doesn't have any self-respect. How are guys going to respect you if you don't respect yourself?"

"Jody, little girl virtue and virginity went out a long time ago. Boys don't care about a girl being a virgin anymore."

"They don't want a big slut, either. You'll see when it comes right down to it; a guy will want a nice girl who hasn't had any sexual experience."

"You can be a nice girl and still have sex. Just because you don't have sex, that doesn't mean you're a good girl, and just because you do that doesn't make you a bad girl."

"I never said it did. I was just talking about how guys feel. They pressure you to have sex with them, and then when it's time for them to get serious, they suddenly realize that there are other girls out there, and it's time they had their freedom."

"Not all guys are like that. If you find someone special and you're both in love, it's only natural that you'll be together, and the guy isn't going to look down on you."

"That's if you find someone really special like that. How many guys do you know who are looking for someone to get to know them and everything? Most of the guys I know are just out trying to get all the action they can."

"I think someone would really have to be special before I had sex with him. I wouldn't just jump into having sex with some guy. I wouldn't trust the guy not to tell all his buddies."

"I want things to be that way too. When Tom and Suzy told me about sex, they said you really should be in love, and everything would be okay. I think if I had sex with any old boy, I would just be going through the motions."

"My parents haven't told me anything about sex. Diane is seventeen, and I bet they haven't talked to her about things either."

"Why don't you ask them something?" she asks. "Maybe they're too embarrassed to bring the subject up."

"Think about how I feel. I'm too embarrassed to ask my parents anything. How old were you when Tom and Suzy told you about the facts of life?"

"I was five when I first started wondering about sex. I had caught my parents making love, and I was curious about what I had seen. They sat me down, and they answered all my questions."

"What did they tell you?"

"Everything."

"Everything? At only five?"

"Sure. If my parents had lied to me then, I probably would have doubted them when they talked to me about sex when I was older."

"Would you believe I just know that two people are supposed to, you know, get together?"

"It's a lot more to it than that," she says. "You should talk to your parents about it."

"I don't know." I pause. "People at school be talking like they know everything, and I am there not knowing anything. I laugh, and I pretend like I know a lot too."

"You had me fooled," she says. "I was going to ask you about things."

"Why? Tom and Suzy have already told you everything."

"It's still nice to talk to someone my own age about it. It's not like I can go up to my parents and tell them I think about having sex."

"I think about it too. I dream a lot about Mark, and sometimes we're together. Maybe that means I'm just horny or something, but it happens a lot."

"I've dreamed like that sometimes too, but it was a faceless boy. Maybe it's because I didn't like anyone then. I don't think it's weird or anything. I guess it's like boys having wet dreams. Nobody says there's anything wrong with them. Why should it be any different for a girl?"

"I don't know," I say. "I guess it's because good

girls aren't supposed to think about having sex."

"Now, look who's talking about girls not being "good,"" she says.

"I didn't say I believed it. It's like a lot of girls I know who are having sex, but they won't go on The Pill. They think it makes them cheap if they're already prepared."

"That's so stupid," she says. "Being on birth control pills is better than ending up pregnant."

"I know that. I'm not going to take any chances. As soon as I fall for a guy, it's time for me to go on The Pill. You never know when you'll give in, and I don't need any baby. My parents would kill me for even thinking about all this."

"I think Suzy would understand," she says. "She would rather I was on The Pill than end up pregnant."

"I guess she would. Seeing how it happened to her."

"Yeah, after only one time, so I'm not stupid enough to believe that you can slip and have sex once and still be safe."

"I will just go to the Eastland Free Clinic to get some help when I'm ready. You know how they're always coming to school to talk to us about Safe Sex and handing out brochures about all the diseases we can catch and everything. We've had that shit drilled into our heads since seventh grade, but I don't think it helps. At least five girls are walking around school pregnant. That's why I'm running to that Free Clinic as fast as I can to get some pills when I fall for some guy, and I think about having sex with him. I'm not worried about all those diseases, but I know I would end up with a stupid baby."

"It's harder now. I heard some girls talking about kids having to have their parents' permission to get help there. Since they gave in to pressure from some religious group."

"That's stupid. Who's going to go to the Eastland Free Clinic if they know their parents are going to find out? I wouldn't. The whole point of even going there was because everything was supposed to be so confidential, and you could trust them not to tell your parents on you. Who even wants to go there if you know your parents will find out and give you a hassle about everything? Sometimes, I think grownups just want to make everything hard for us. They tell us to be responsible and do the right thing. Then they make it impossible for us to even do that. All this shit is so messed up, and I know I would never go to someplace like that if my parents had to find out, so I don't know what I'm going to do now."

"It really sucks, doesn't it? I feel like kids have no rights. Sometimes, it's like everything is against us. Maybe we do grow up too fast sometimes, but nobody can keep us as little kids, by denying us access to the health care we need to make everything all right. Remember the fuss the parents made when the Eastland Free Clinic handed out condoms last month? Don't they read the paper or hear the News? Kids are having sex. Not letting us have some protection isn't going to prevent it."

"My dad would kill me if he knew, so I'll have to find a way around it."

"I trust Suzy enough to confide in her. I think she'd be glad I was honest with her and grateful that I'm not taking any chances. It would be hard talking to Tom about something like that, though. I'll always be his little girl. He wouldn't want to think about me being with some guy."

"I wish I could talk to my mother, but it's so hard. She makes me feel like she doesn't care about my problems, and she'd probably make me feel dirty. Like there's something wrong with me for having sex with a guy."

"I just wish so many diseases weren't out there that make everything so scary," Jody says. "It's so hard to be a teenager and not worry about all that. It's like every disease you can think of can happen if you don't use a condom. Every day we get that Safe Sex stuff drilled into our heads, but it's like nobody is even listening."

"I listen, but I'm not worried about all that. Have you ever heard about anybody around here getting AIDS or anything like that? Besides, Carsonville is so small, and just about everybody knows each other. Can you imagine something like AIDS happening here?"

"Well, I'm from New York, and I've seen the disease close up," Jody says. "I think it can happen anywhere."

"You worry too much," I tell her. "There are about two hundred million people in America. Carsonville has less than twenty-five thousand people living here. What are the chances of somebody getting something like AIDS? Especially a teenager. I think the odds are in our favor."

"Well, I can't stop worrying just like that. AIDS is such an epidemic around the world, and it affects everybody. I just think about all those unlucky people who have gotten sick over the years because they didn't practice Safe Sex, and it gets to me. I think that suffering from a disease like AIDS is such an awful, cruel way to die."

"We're fourteen," I say. "Who can even think about dying? We haven't even started to live yet."

"Let's talk about this later," she decides. "Aren't you hungry?"

"Yeah, I'm hungry, but this whole subject is so interesting. It's nice to be able to quit pretending and just level about what you're really feeling. I really have a lot of fears. You know, like, will I be ready?"

"You should have that talk with your parents."

"I'll think about it. You don't know how hard it is reaching my parents. Mom would probably think I've already done something, and she'd say something to make me feel guilty anyway. Dad probably wouldn't talk about it at all."

"Things will work out."

"They can't get any worse."

We switch subjects as soon as we are out of her room. Her parents are great, but we don't want them to know what we were discussing. It's after eleven and a little late for breakfast, but I guess everything will be okay.

CHAPTER 11

Ricky has been a lot nicer to me since that night we met at Cassidy's, three weeks ago, but I know we still have a long way to go. He can have anybody he wants, and he knows it. Besides, Cathy Rankin still has him. They've been going steady since summer and showing no signs of breaking up. What makes me think I have a chance is beyond me.

Maybe it's because I have him puzzled. I keep being suggestive, but I'm distant at the same time. He doesn't know where my head is. That's probably what keeps him interested. Usually, girls just lay it out in the open, and he knows he can do what he pleases. I've let him know he can't treat me like that.

We've been saying "Hi" to each other every time we pass in the halls, and the other day, he stood outside Study Hall, and he talked to me until the bell rang. I think Cathy has started to notice the attention he pays to me, but that smug, self-assured look never leaves her face. I guess she thinks I can't measure up to her and so she doesn't have anything to worry about.

Since Ricky has been paying attention to me, some of the other top guys at school have started to notice me too. I'm used to regular guys like Mark talking to me, but some influential guys have started being interested in me. I guess they figure if a guy like Ricky is giving me some of his time, I must have something to offer. I haven't gotten asked out yet, but I'm hopeful. I'm tired of sitting at home every weekend. There's nothing to do. Except help my mother clean up the house, or I could start babysitting. That's what girls do who don't have a social life. That sounds very boring to me.

I want to go out on dates and go to parties. Anything! Besides, spend the next four years being a "straight." That's what they call the kids who don't do anything, and you feel like a misfit. I want to belong. I'd do anything to fit in. I'm not like Jody. I care about being accepted.

I finally believe that Jody doesn't want to be popular. After the Follies, Jody had all kinds of girls trying to be her friend. I wasn't there, but I heard she really did a great job. And these important girls were asking her questions about her date and wanting to know who French-braided her hair. Jody had her ticket to everything, popularity, and everything that goes with it. And do you know what she did? Jody stood by me. She said they're all a bunch of phonies and that's why she likes me. Because I speak what's really on my mind and I don't try to be something I'm not.

I don't know if I would have done that. I like Jody, and she's my best friend, but I don't know if I would choose popularity over her. I would like to think I wouldn't, but it's been so important to me for so long. I would like to think I could do both. Be accepted and keep all my old friends. I don't want to forget everything else and be so stuck on myself that I think I can make it alone.

Jody didn't want the popularity, but my plan worked. Mitch asked her out. They've gone out tonight. They're supposed to go to a movie and end up at Pop Tofflers afterward for Cokes. Jody said she would call me when she gets home to give me the news or if it's too late, she'll wait until tomorrow.

I hope it will be too late. That will mean that Jody's having fun. I had to convince her to go in the first place. She was going to turn down a chance of a lifetime because of one fear. Mitch doesn't know she's half-black, and anyway, it shouldn't even matter. I think she's getting a complex about it. Jody has the conversational thing under wraps. Jody has been talking more around the school, and she stood up for herself towards Linda and her friends.

I was shocked. Jody got in Linda's face, and she told the bitch where she could go. I think Linda just picked on Jody because she thought Jody was scared of her. When Jody stood up to Linda and was acting like Jody was going to start some shit, Linda backed down.

I didn't want people walking all over Jody. I could have done something about the situation myself. But Jody doesn't need me fighting her battles, and I thought it was time she showed the kids at school that she wasn't a doormat that they could walk all over.

Jody has straightened herself out, and I'm trying to straighten myself out. Jody thinks I should have a talk with my folks. Not just about sex, but about everything. I wish I could, but I don't want to be rejected. If your parents have always been there for you, then you don't know what it's like not to have parental support.

I feel like if I got in trouble or made a mistake, my parents wouldn't be there for me to lean on. I know from past experiences that I can't count on them to defend me or even support me when I'm down. Families should stick together through thick and thin, but Family is just a word as far as we're concerned. I've always known that they weren't going to be there for me.

When I was little, I threw a lot of temper tantrums to get their attention, but I'm too old for that now. Crying and screaming isn't going to help anything. If I want to get treated like an adult, I need to act like one. But what's the use of behaving maturely if your parents still think you're a stupid kid and they treat you that way?

The phone rings. I go answer it. I bet it's for Diane. It's like her friends can sense when she's at home, and they spend half the night tying up our lines. Nobody else has a chance to use the phone. It's tough when you only have one telephone line. “Hello.”

“Hi, it's me.”

“You're back early, aren't you?” I glance at the clock. “It's only 10:17.”

“We figured since it was a school night, we wouldn't stay out too late.”

“Did you have fun?”

“It was all right.” She pauses. “He didn't try anything.”

“You sound disappointed.”

“I am - a little. I was beginning to wonder if something was wrong with me or something.”

“And if he had tried something, you would have been offended.”

“I guess. It's just that you expect it from a guy. I was ready to turn him down easily, and he didn't try anything.”

“Hmmm.”

“He asked me out again for Friday night.”

“He did?” I ask. “That's great.”

“It's okay, but I'm not getting serious. I like Russ too.”

“You haven't talked about him for a long time.”

"That's because you always act like he's the lowest," she reminds me. "Just because he's a freshman."

"I never said anything about him being low."

"I knew how you felt." She pauses again. "I didn't want to tell you, but I guess if I don't, you'll kill me. Ricky asked about you."

"He did?"

"Yeah, he's a friend of Mitch's, and he sat at the table with us for a while. He said, 'How's your hot friend, Angel?' I got ticked off at first, but then I tried to build you up."

"You did that for me?"

"Yeah, you're my friend, aren't you?"

"Your best friend."

"So anyway, Ricky asked me if I thought you'd go out with him."

"If I'd go out with him!"

"Yeah, and I said, 'Why don't you ask her?' and he said, 'I will,' so I guess he will."

"A date with Ricky Flecher," I say. "I can't believe it."

"Hey, can I call you back tomorrow?"

"Sure, but what's wrong?"

"Suzy is waiting for all the details. I only called to let you know about Ricky. I knew you'd want to know about that tonight."

"Thanks, Jody. Bye."

I hang up.

A date with Ricky Flecher. That's what I've always wanted. Maybe things are starting to turn around for me. I don't think about Cathy Rankin. I start daydreaming about going out with Ricky and getting accepted finally.

CHAPTER 12

Carsonville is still like a small town to me, but it has grown steadily in the past several years. The Mill is in the center of our township, and everything else expands from it. Downtown, there's not much activity, but there are still some businesses willing to stay in the area. On Main street, there's the Dime Store, which takes up three-quarters of a city block. Next to it is Nancy's Dress Shop. Across the street is Decker Bookstore, the original Lib's Cookies and Aunt Becky's Sandwiches, which has the best subs in town.

There are various other Shops and Businesses which occupy the surrounding streets. Some have steady customers who don't mind coming downtown to shop. Others just barely stay open with the few customers they get daily. The only time I go to that area is once a month, on a Saturday morning, when I visit my grandmother at Oaktown Nursing Home. Nan has been staying at that place since my grandfather died three years ago, and my parents didn't think she could survive at home, but they didn't want her to live with us. Nan is always thankful for my monthly visits, and she cheers up. After every visit with Nan, I always stop at Aunt Becky's Sandwiches to eat a Meatball Sub. Then I go next door to get a couple of oatmeal raisin cookies at Lib's Cookies.

Mostly, everyone goes to the two big Malls, Northland and Greentree, to shop or either to the Strip Mall, Cassidy's. Downtown was a lot busier before they built those Malls. Most businesses followed the Malls to the Northside of town and left those faithful downtown businesses to fail, but they just seem to hang on year after year. I know I prefer going to the Malls too and I spend a lot of time there. Things are not hurried downtown, and the service is better and friendlier. Still, I guess sometimes customers can overlook excellent customer service like that.

I have only lived in Carsonville for about five years, and it's bigger than my last hometown, Vicksburg, but sometimes I feel suffocated here. It's like nothing ever changes. Folks are used to things being a certain way, and they never want anything to be different. Yes, we have the Malls now, and a lot more people have moved to our town, but it's like it's still the same old small town it always was.

There are nine big businesses in Carsonville. The Mill, Rankin Enterprises, Forrester Insurance, where my dad works, Crystal Plasma, Indiana Bell, Southern Indiana Gas and Electric Company, Carsonville Water Works, Carsonville Cable, and Bolden Investments. Thousands of people worked at The Mill before they had that workers strike and laid off a big chunk of its workforce once the strike was settled. Now, a lot of families are suffering, and there doesn't seem much hope for the local economy. I guess Crystal Plasma is extra busy because a lot of people have to sell their plasma weekly just to try to get by. Dad complains about people sacrificing things like Life Insurance to make ends meet. It keeps him upset since his customer base's fear of taking care of the family after death is his livelihood.

Nobody really knows what those big shots at Rankin Enterprises do. Its success depends on outsiders, so nobody gives the company much thought. Cathy Rankin loves to brag that her father owns the company, and Linda Thomas claims her father is a Vice President there. The electric company, the water company, the telephone company, and cable company will survive no matter how bad the economy gets. Still, a lot of folks worry about being able to keep up their payments. Bolden Investments sprung up out of nowhere last winter. It seems like a beacon of hope to a lot of people. I've heard Dad and his friends bragging about the significant checks they've received from their investments in the company. They talk about how they would like to pass on their good fortune to even more people in the community.

Those nine companies have buildings that stand tall in Carsonville. Rankin Enterprises building is a skyscraper, and it seems out of place in our town. The Mill stretches over several acres, and there's always a steady hum of machinery. Even when the strike was going on, those in management kept the machines going, and the hum was never silenced. Sometimes at night, I have nightmares of working at The Mill for life, and I always break out in a cold sweat. Most of the people around here would think that lifelong employment at The Mill was a dream come true.

On the west side of town, there's a lot of land and

nobody has really bothered to develop anything out there. Maybe six or seven people have big, rambling houses that sit on acres of land, but mostly it's nothing. There's always talk about Developers coming in and doing something with all that available land. Still, so far, nothing has come out of it. Sometimes Dad and his friends go out there, and they hunt for rabbits and deers. Once, when we first moved here, Dad ran into one of those deers, and it messed the front of our car up. Of course, Dad had insurance, so it really wasn't a problem. I haven't been to the Westside since then.

The Eastside is more developed, and it has been booming lately. There are several new apartment complexes and fancy developments with huge houses, which sell for at least $500,000. Also, there's Walmart and all the new businesses it has attracted. You go to the Eastside of town, and you see newness. New enterprises, luxury apartments, and expensive houses. It's nicknamed The New Carsonville, and it's mostly people new to Carsonville who live out there. Gale Stewart lives in one of those new housing developments. Her family can afford to because her father is President of Carsonville Bank. There are about five branches of the bank, but her father controls things at the old Colonial building near the riverfront.

Once you leave downtown, you have to go through the Southside of town to get back to the Northside. There's a big Projects complex that takes up a lot of space and small neighborhoods that surround it. There are various businesses you can see as you ride the Lincoln Avenue bus back and forth from downtown to Northland Mall. I've never given much thought to the southside until lately. I guess it's because those three hundred black kids came from

Lincoln High School, and I was surrounded by black kids at Central for the first time in my life. I know everything is so run-down on the southside, and you can see boarded buildings and some houses that look like they should be condemned. Even with the whir of the bus speeding by, I can see all the graffiti on the Projects building and stomped away grass with trash in almost every yard. It's not much past noon, but little kids are running around unsupervised, and some adult sare standing around, looking like they have nothing going on for themselves. You can definitely tell how bad things are for those people.

I'm not like Gale Stewart and anxious to walk around the southside like it's nothing. Everybody in town hears about all the violence that's associated with that part of town. Even as tough as I am, I wouldn't want to put myself into a situation I couldn't handle. I suppose if I made a black friend that lived on the southside and she invited me over to her house, I would go (in the daytime), but that's about it. Jody is hanging around this black girl named Cindy Higgins on the girls' basketball team, and she says she'll probably go over to her house. Jody is so brave lately, and she's changing so much, but I know she's still the same in all the important ways.

Houses start getting better, and the whole atmosphere changes as you pass the highway and you get to the Northside of town. Successful businesses start popping up and more expensive houses. I live on an ordinary block called Dearborn Avenue, and Jody lives just two blocks before that on a better street called Berkley Drive. We can both walk to school because Central is just five blocks down from my house. I get off the bus at the corner, and I head home. I never tell anybody that I visit Nan so much. It's just something between her and me. My parents and Diane probably think I've forgotten her at Oaktown the way they have.

After I've relaxed in my room awhile, I start thinking about tonight's basketball game against North Terrace. They are our biggest rivals. They love to come to town to beat us on our own turf. Sometimes it's like they will always win, and I know tonight won't be an exception. North Terrace knows they are better than us, and we will never defeat them. North Terrace is just a small town about 15 miles away. Only, it's more country, and those kids grow big. I've only been there once. Jody and I had Tom drive there for a football game that was actually a home game. I could tell by looking at their school building that it was a lot like Central.

Central has been around since the fifties, but it looks new compared to Lincoln. There has been a lot of updates on the building and constant upkeep to make sure everything stays modern. It's like nobody cared about Lincoln, and that's why it was so rundown. I've never really given much thought to my school. The red brick building is big and sturdy, filled with numerous bright classrooms and a large cafeteria, which just about everybody eats at during the three lunch periods, and the two Gyms. The Girls' Gym is much smaller than the Boys' Gym, and all the volleyball and basketball games are held in the Boys' Gym.

There are bleachers at the bottom of the Boys' Gym. The Juniors sit at the right, and the seniors sit at the left. There are stairs to the upper section. The freshmen sit on the left, and the sophomores sit at the right. There are over two thousand students who attend Central, and there's enough room for everybody. When there's a Pep Assembly, like the one held yesterday, the gym is always rocking with kids cheering on the team. During games, it's especially loud since Central's fans have a lot of school spirit. I know that's hard because our teams usually lose, and we have to cheer for them anyway. I scream hard for the boys' varsity basketball team, and it's hard to see Mark just sitting the bench like always, but it doesn't affect my good mood.

I always think my life is so pathetic, and I have my share of teen angst, but I suppose things could be a lot worst. I know I dream a lot about escaping to a big city, so I will finally have some excitement in my life. I get scared that I wouldn't know what to do once I was out of a small town. I'm only fourteen, and I have four years left before I graduate from Central. There's a lot of time to think about my future. My worst fear, though, is that I'll just get stuck in Carsonville for life and never escape at all. I get a cold chill, and I try to lose myself in the basketball game between Central and North Terrace.

CHAPTER 13

It might surprise everyone that I like to cook. I'm always experimenting in the kitchen, and most of my creations are edible. I always bake five dozen chocolate chip cookies to take to Nan at Oaktown to share with the other residents at the nursing home. Most of those elderly people can't have any sugar, so I've come up with unique ways to sweeten the cookies, but I'm not giving away my recipes. Dad doesn't have much good to say about me, but he does admire the meals I always cook. I guess him appreciating my cooking skills is something.

I know I complain about my dad's distance so much, and I worry that he doesn't want to be bothered with me, but that's just because I want to be closer to him. I always say I hate my parents, and I don't want to be bothered with them either. I'm so lame that I do want a relationship with Mom and Dad. I look at Dad, and I see a lot of myself in him. I'm only 5"2, and I get some of my height from him. Dad's only about 5"5. Mom is even shorter than me at 5"0. I feel like a shrimp sometimes, because Jody is 5"11. It's funny how Jody's so much taller than me, but she looks up to me.

Even if our parents hadn't told us she was adopted, I guess Diane and I would have realized that something in our genes didn't match. Diane is 5"8, she's so pretty, naturally blond and still would be smart if it wasn't for the weed numbing her brain. I look at my sister, and I stay jealous of her. I know the only reason I bleach my own hair blond is to be like her. My hair grows so fast, and sometimes you can see my black roots. Dad is totally gray, but Mom has black hair like me, with only streaks of grayness. Mom used to dye her hair every two weeks, but one day she woke up, and she decided to let nature take its course. I see pictures of the four of us, and it's like we're nothing alike, and I guess it's true because we couldn't be more different.

I'm always saying Jody is so beautiful, and she is. Jody has a sandy shade of hair that she lets hang long down her back. When she smiles, she has dimples and her nose twitches. Jody's skin is so smooth, and I don't think she has ever had any pimples. My mom would call her a classic beauty because she only wears lipstick and mascara, so make-up isn't responsible for her good looks. Sometimes, I look at Jody, and I wonder why I couldn't have been born beautiful like that. I know I'm such a pretty girl, but when I'm with Jody, all the guys' eyes are focused on her, and I might as well be a toad or totally invisible.

The only two guys I really care about are Ricky Flecher and Mark Davis, and I just like flirting with all the rest of the guys. Both boys are jocks who made the Varsity Football team and the Varsity Basketball team. They're both tall, blond, and built. Only, Ricky has a handsome face like a male model, and Mark is good-looking in an average sort of way. Most of the girls at school try to chase Ricky down, and a lot of freshmen girls are always checking Mark out. Mark has finally stopped picking at his pimples, and his zits are clearing up. Maybe he'll get the mustache he wants soon, and he'll continue to grow his hair out, so it's past his shoulders. Ricky looks like he could be on the cover of a Teen magazine, and having all those girls swoon over him has made him so cocky.

Ricky is like the perfect guy you can never have, but you will never stop wanting him. I look into Ricky's eyes sometimes, and I get lost. It's been almost two months since I first met him at Cassidy's, and I try very hard to just talk to him like a regular person and not be out to impress him, but it's hard. It's so much easier to talk to Mark, and I feel relaxed about sharing everything with him – except the most important thing. I like Ricky so much, but I think I'm in love with Mark.

It's like there are so many faces at Central, and mostly everyone gets lost in the crowd. Jody stands out because of her beauty. The popular kids are known to everybody, so they don't fade into the background either. I try to make myself be on display too. That's why I wore those Daisy Dukes shorts that time and left the house without a bra on and was falling all over the guys. I get attention from some guys, but I wanted to get noticed even more. I like teasing guys, and I know everyone thinks I'm such a flirt, but I haven't come close to pleasing some guy.

I see how Gale brags about her sex life to anybody who will listen at school, and everybody puts her down. Mark is a guy, and guys like to brag about their own sexual exploits, but he was put off by Gale acting that way. I think his attitude is funny. I would never tell anybody about my own sex life if I actually had one. Still, I think it takes a lot of guts for Gale to put it on the line like that. People would say Gale was lying if she tried to act innocent anyway, so why shouldn't Gale brag like that?

I think Gale would have had a lot of attention from guys anyway. Even if she hadn't started having sex with anybody who would buy her a Big Mac and a Shake, because she's so pretty. Gale has sad eyes that get lost in her pale face. Gale's not a vampire, so I don't know why she doesn't like getting any sun. Her blond hair flows down her back, and Gale always keeps it held back with black hair clips on each side of her head.

It's like when you talk to Gale, she has all the confidence in the world, and she can control any situation. It's just that her eyes stay so sad, and it's like something is ticking in her head that nobody knows about. Gale is always prancing around, and she's such a force that she seems a lot taller than 5"4. Gale is so popular. She stays on everybody's lips, and everything seems to always go her way. Maybe I'm just imagining that there's something in her eyes.

I always wish I could be like Gale. Not the easiest slut at the school part, but having everyone know who I am. Sometimes, it's like I will always be on the outside looking in on the important people at school. I feel like I will never be accepted for how I am, and I try my best to change into the person they want. I know I can be so aggressive, and a lot of people are scared of me. I've been trying to control my temper lately, and this is the longest time I've gone without having a fight. I let shit slide, and I act like I haven't gotten pissed off. Nobody knows how hard it is to act civil and not just go off on somebody. I wish I could just behave like all the other girls at school.

I look at those other girls, and I wonder what it would be like just to be so passive. Most of the girls blend together, and it's hard to look at them as individuals. Maybe some of those girls try hard to make that impression. Nobody wants to stand out over something stupid. I'm not happy in the background, and I'm always pushing myself to be on center stage, but I would like to be unique too. Maybe I'm too secure in m yown identity, and I always walk around as if nothing can touch me. I really wish I could allow other people besides Jody close enough to break through my armor. I shut everybody out, though, and I keep them wondering what I'm about.

I get so mad sometimes about my position at school, and I think about how other kids have things. Nobody could be as miserable as me. I see how Jody has started blooming. It's like after The Follies, Jody had popularity in her hands, and it was like she could have things the way I've always wanted them to be for me. I watched her walk around Central like a different girl and how everyone accepted her that way. Jody talks more to the kids around the school, she's always dating Mitch O'Connors, and she's making a lot of other friends. Jody's captain of the girls' varsity basketball team, but I know she doesn't want to be popular. Jody talks about The Phonies at school all the time, and she says various things about how much she detests the very kids I'm dying to get noticed by.

I ache to belong, and Jody just tosses it away like it doesn't even matter. I can't understand that. Jody is so confident with the basketball, and she's been leading the Lady Bears to victory. I see how she's taking charge like that, and it makes me want to try harder too. Sports are out. I listen to the bulletin every morning, and I hear about the various clubs and activities available. I never try to participate in anything, though. Maybe I am responsible for my own misery. If I wanted the popularity so much, then I would get involved at school to go after it. I can't expect to get acceptance handed to me like it was to Jody.

I know a lot of kids at school, and I'm on speaking terms with them. Some freshmen kids. Maybe I just want to get involved with the top kids at Central. I see how everyone gives out of their way for those kids, and I wish I could have things be that way for me. I watch Cathy Rankin and Sheila Haskle, and it's like neither one of them has to suffer any teen angst. Sheila was Homecoming Queen for the football team, and she's so bubbly and outgoing, and she's friendly towards everybody. Cathy is the complete opposite of her. Cathy's quick to put somebody down, and she acts like she hates the other kids at school for even existing. Cathy is in the "in" group, and they're the top clique at school. Maybe Sheila is only in the second most popular clique, but I believe that Shelia has more power than Cathy.

There are about two hundred popular kids at Central, and they have such attitudes. Still, those are the kids that I'm gravitating towards. I want to be one of THEM. I want people to hear the name Angel Moore and have it mean something to them. I walk around all unhappy because I can't be a top girl. I always act like it's not enough that I have good friends like Jody and Mark, and I get along with a lot of regular kids like me. I know I couldn't take over at Central just like that, but I worry that it will never happen. There are seniors at school who are still at the bottom of the popularity ladder. After four years at Central, they're still nobodies, and they don't even matter. I want to be at the top of that ladder someday and really be influential and make my mark.

Things like that are important at Central. Everybody wants to be the top dog, and nobody wants to be a lowly loser. Everybody fights to get to that top rung on the popularity ladder. Most of us are stuck on the bottom rung, with a few on the middle rungs, and only a select group at the top rung. I'm fighting to get past the middle rungs and landing at the very top rung. I feel like it's going to be hard to propel myself like that, but I will never give up on trying. I just hope I don't crash to the ground and only burn instead.

CHAPTER 14

School has been going okay. My grades aren't that terrific, but everything else is okay. During Math, I stare at the back of Mark's head. How can you stop feeling something you don't want to feel? I wish I still thought of Mark as only a friend. At least when I told myself that, I wasn't so miserable.

Everything should be going okay for me, but a thing like this had to happen. I know I'm in love with Mark. I've never felt like this about a boy before. Usually, I just think a guy is cute, and I act flirty until the next one comes along. With Mark, it's different. I like being around him, and I daydream about us a lot.

It's hard having so many classes together. I need to pretend that everything is the way it's always been. I want to tell him how I feel, but I'm scared he'll believe that everybody was right from the start. That I only got close to him so I could steal him away. If that happened, I wouldn't have a friendship or anything.

Besides, I'm not too sure he wouldn't think I was joking. If he laughed in my face, I'd die of embarrassment. I have a feeling something like that would happen. Mark doesn't take me seriously. He only thinks of me as one of the guys. I'm the one Mark tells his problems to. He even talks about his girlfriend to me. I'm the one who started that, but I wish Mark would stop talking about Linda to me. There I am feeling something for him, and he's talking about her.

I talk about other guys to cover up for how I feel. I trust Mark, but I don't want to test him. I don't tell him a lot about myself. The biggest thing I can't confess to him. I've imagined telling him that I love him, and it always works out okay. But I know things don't happen like that in real life.

"What's wrong, Angel?" Mark asks.

"What do you mean?"

"You're not talking."

"What do you want to talk about, Davis?"

"Why did you call me Davis? Usually, it's Mark."

"Does it even matter?"

"Not really. What have you been up to lately?"

"Same as usual."

"Have you been hitting on any new guys?"

"Nah, Ricky's been taking up all my time."

"Oh."

"Have you heard? Jody is going out with Mitch O'Connors."

"That jerk, he's as bad as Ricky Flecher."

"If I didn't know any better, I'd think you were jealous."

"I'm not. I don't care who you hit on."

I don't say anything. I can't talk for the lump in my throat. I'm glad I haven't told Mark how I feel. He's told me how he feels without me even asking him. He didn't have to do that. He could have let me have my dreams.

When the bell rings, I walk out of the room without saying a word to Mark. He makes me so sick. He should know how I feel. Jody is always telling me that she knows he likes me, but I know it's not true. He doesn't care anything about me.

"Hey, Angel, wait up!"

I stop.

Ricky catches up to me. He puts his arm around me, and for the first time, I put my arm around him. We laugh, and we joke around. We get a lot of stares. I don't care what anybody thinks. I'm out for myself, and I do what I please. Who cares what everyone thinks? I ask Ricky out in a roundabout way, and he stops.

"Are you asking me out?"

"Not really."

"Good. I like to be the one who does the asking."

"What are you waiting on then?"

"Didn't your friend tell you what I said?"

"Who? Jody?"

"Yeah, the one who goes out with Mitch O'Connors."

"Yeah, she told me. But you never did anything about it."

"I didn't know whether you would go. How about it? You want to go out tonight?"

"Sure, why not?"

"If I had known it would be this easy, I'd have asked you out ages ago."

"I wish you would have." I look at him. "What about Cathy?"

"What about her?"

"She's not going to like us going out."

"Who says she has to know?"

"As long as you don't get in trouble."

"I can handle Cathy."

"I'm sure you can."

"I'll pick you up about seven." I give him my address, and he writes it down. "I'll see you later."

He walks off.

I should be happy. It's finally happened. I have a date with Ricky Flecher. It's funny, but all the excitement isn't there. I keep thinking about Mark. I try to shake it off. He doesn't matter. Ricky is ten times better than him. I need to start thinking about what's important.

CHAPTER 15

Dad doesn't give me a hassle about getting asked out on a school night. Mom is full of questions. I get the impression that she doesn't trust me. She'll probably want to know every detail when I get home. Not because she's happy I had a good time and she wants to share it with me. But because she just wants to make sure I haven't done anything wrong. Sometimes, I really wish I had parents I could talk to and that they tried to understand me, but Mom and Dad act like they just do their duty, and they're never there for me when I really need them.

Ricky comes on time, and in the car, we don't talk that much. I'm nervous. You would think I've never been out with a guy before. I've had a couple of dates, but not with a guy as influential as Ricky. He seems at ease. I guess he just has something else on his mind. I can't imagine a guy like Ricky being uptight about a date.

At Pop Tofflers, we draw a lot of attention. As

soon as we enter the door, a lot of girls stare at us. I can feel those eyes following us to the booth. I bet Cathy already knows we're here. I feel excited about the whole thing. I think a lot of those girls are envious of me. Ricky just doesn't go out with any girl. You need to be pretty and exceptional and a top girl at school, so knowing that he picked me fills me with a lot of confidence, and it makes me feel good about myself.

Ricky orders Cokes and burgers for us. I guess all that attention boosts my ego. I want to show him I'm a good date. We joke around, and it's like the times at school. I try hard to impress Ricky, and he's his old cocky self. Maybe when I really get to know him, I'll finally act like myself. Not tried to show him that I'm not a little kid.

I'm fourteen, but I don't want to be treated like a kid. I want to be grown up. That's why I go out of my way to prove that I'm not a little kid anymore. I think I matured faster than some of the kids around me, and I want to be treated like I am mature.

We're laughing and joking around, but it's not that much fun. The date is really kind of boring. I always thought it would be filled with so much excitement that my heart would be beating fast. But the only thing that makes it fun is the fact that all those girls keep looking over at us and I can tell that they're jealous. That's a heck of a way to feel about your date with the best-looking boy at school.

"Ricky, are you having fun?" I ask.

"Do you want to know the truth?"

"I thought so."

"Do you want to take a drive?"

"Sure, why not?"

Ricky pays for our order, and we go out to the car. Ricky has a black Corvette. He said he got it for his sixteenth birthday. I'd hate to see what Ricky gets when the guy graduates from high school. I bet he gets whatever he wants. Maybe that's why he's so used to having things his way.

"Well, what do you want to do?" he asks after we've been driving awhile.

"Anything you want."

"You may not like what I have in mind."

"I'm sure I will."

"I'll be happy to spend a little time with you. If you know what I mean."

I do. It's funny, but I don't even care. The one boy I love doesn't even care about me. I should be happy that someone like Ricky wants to spend some time with me. Any of those girls at Pop Tofflers would be thrilled to get a chance like this.

Ricky parks at Huffington Beach. We get out of the car, and he goes back to the trunk. He gets a blanket out. Boy, he comes prepared. Now that the time has come, I've gotten nervous. My knees are shaking, and my heart is beating over time. I want to tell Ricky to take me home, but I'm scared of what he'll say.

We start walking along. Ricky has my hand, and I know my palms are sweaty. I think I'm going to start crying or something. I need to build my nerves up. I keep telling myself that I never cared about being a virgin. I'm not like Jody. Little girl virtue and virginity never meant anything to me. Sure, I wanted to be in love with the guy and everything. Does that even matter at a time like this?

Ricky stops by the pier. There are about fifty million rocks to climb to get to the top. I'm sure with my jelly legs, I'm going to fall. Ricky still has my hand, and I follow along after him. I'm sure he's not nervous about anything.

When we get to the top of the pier, Ricky spreads the blanket out, and we sit down. At least I won't get sprinters. He kisses me on the cheek, and then he pulls me into his arms. We kiss awhile. I don't kiss him back. Not really. He eases me down on the blanket, and he uses his hands more.

"What's wrong?" he asks.

"Nothing."

"Why aren't you responding, then?"

"I am. You just can't tell."

Ricky kisses me again. I try to respond. Funny thoughts keep running through my mind. I don't think about what is about to happen. I think about school. How things are going to be different now that I'm Ricky's girl. I keep imagining myself being popular.

"I love your body - it's beautiful."

"Is it really beautiful?"

"Yeah, it's driving me crazy," he says in a raspy voice.

When his voice is low like that, it sounds just like Mark's. I can't describe all the feelings that flow through me after I've imagined Mark saying and doing all that to me. I get turned on, and I start kissing Ricky back. He wants more. I'm out of my clothes, and I don't even try to stop him. I don't think I could if I tried.

Ricky gets out of his clothes too, and I try to catch a deep breath. He is built well, and when I look at that, I get scared again, because even if I've never seen any other one before, I know his thing is big. I'm not that wet, and I know he can really hurt me if he wants to. I pray to myself that he will be gentle because he knows I'm only fourteen, and it's my first time. It does hurt, and I try to pull away from him, but he just holds me there. I want to cry so badly, but I won't let the tears come, and I try to make myself numb enough to take me away from the whole thing, so I won't even have to think about it anymore. At least the pain goes away after a while, and I know I can take it. I'm a strong girl, and I'm not going to act like a baby about sex, and I won't do anything to embarrass myself, because it's not that bad.

It's not like I thought it would be. All I knew was that two people are supposed to get together. Sometimes I feel so dumb because everyone else knows all about doing it, and I'm just learning. I wanted the love and everything that goes with it, but sometimes you need to give up on fantasies and deal with the real world. Love is a lie, and all you do is get hurt, so it's better just to be with someone who at least likes you and is willing to spend some time with you to show you. Ricky knows what he's doing, but he isn't doing anything for me. I just lie there. I even stop thinking about Mark. He doesn't care anything about me anyway, and it is wrong to do something like that to Ricky. He's giving it his all and I'm thinking about another guy. I guess all those sports built up his endurance. He doesn't get tired that easily, and I don't think it will ever end. Still, I pray that it's soon, because my legs are starting to cramp, and this wooden pier isn't exactly the most comfortable place to get slammed into.

Afterward, I get dressed, and I go over to the edge of the pier. I won't look at Ricky. I stare down at the water, and I have this huge lump in my throat. I can't believe I went out with a guy one time, and I acted like a complete slut. I wonder if he's busy thinking that I'm such a skank bitch and wishing that he had never even got with me in the first place. I feel so ashamed, and I wish I had never done it. I'm so invincible, and I always hide my true feelings, so I try to keep my uneasiness to myself. I don't know what to say. Maybe there isn't anything to utter at a time like this.

Ricky comes over, and he sits down beside me. He acts like he doesn't know what to say either. I still can't believe I went ahead, and I did it with a guy that I hardly know.

I don't feel love towards Ricky. Not love or anything else. I keep thinking he's just another guy, and there is nothing at all special about him. Maybe he scores more, but that's the only difference.

“What's wrong with you?” he wants to know.

“There's nothing wrong with me.”

“Why are you acting so funny?”

“I'm not acting funny,” I lie. “I just don't know what to say.”

“Did you come?”

“Did you?”

“Sure, but I was asking about you.”

“I don't know. I've never done that before.”

“You were a virgin!” he says in a shocked voice. “I can't believe it.”

“What did you expect?” I ask. “I'm only fourteen.”

“I thought you'd been around.”

“Does that even matter now?” I ask. “When will

I see you again?"

"Well, I'm going out on dates all weekend with Cathy," he says. "Maybe I can squeeze you in for Monday night."

"You act like I have to make an appointment to get laid."

"Well..."

"Well, nothing. Take me home."

I'm furious. I won't say anything to Ricky as we walk towards the car. I went and did something like that because I was angry with Mark and I wanted to get even. I should have been smarter, but I'm not going to get a scholarship with my smarts.

CHAPTER 16

I head over to Jody's house before I go home. I don't care about being out past my curfew. I really need somebody to talk to, and Jody is the only one who won't be judgmental and nothing else. I know a best friend is the only one who will understand. I can't wait to get to her room and tell her everything.

"How did your date go?" she asks.

"What date? We just went to Huffington Beach, and we made out. I'm so stupid. He was giving me all this bullshit about what a beautiful body I have and everything."

"You didn't go all the way, did you?"

"What do you think? Can't you tell by the way I'm walking? I thought everybody would be able to tell."

"You can't tell a thing like that," she assures me. "Quit worrying."

"When I asked him when I'd see him again, he said he'll be busy with Cathy, and Ricky'll have to let me know when he can work me into his schedule."

"They are going steady."

"That doesn't matter. Ricky should have been thinking about her before he fucked me."

"I tried to tell you how Ricky is."

"I know, but I thought things could be different. I didn't even want to do anything tonight, but I was too scared to tell Ricky that. You know how we were talking that time and saying how we wanted it to be? I really wanted it to be that way."

"Everything will be all right. Ricky probably won't tell anyone. Nobody has to know."

"Knowing him, he'll tell all the guys."

"I don't think he will do anything like that. He's a jerk, but he would have to be pretty low to sink to that."

"I don't care," I sniff. "Ricky Flecher can just go to Hell!"

"I hope you're not pregnant."

"I'm so stupid. I shouldn't have taken that chance. I should have known Ricky wouldn't use protection."

"You better go get checked out."

"It wouldn't show up this soon. I'm getting on

The Pill anyway. I'm not taking any more chances."

"You're going to have to tell your parents."

"No way. Mom would never give her permission for me to go on The Pill. I'm going to have to find a way around it."

"Suzy took me to her gynecologist, and I just had to have a pelvic exam. It's that simple."

"When did you go on The Pill?"

"About two months ago."

"Why didn't you tell me?" I demand. "I'm supposed to be your best friend."

"It's something private. I talked about it with Suzy and everything, but I didn't know how to tell you about it. Suzy was understandable about it. I thought she would be the one upset, but Tom took it hard. He doesn't like the idea of me growing up so fast, but he doesn't judge me."

"You lost your virginity, and you didn't even tell me. I tell you everything. Well, almost everything."

"It was really great. Russ and I talked afterward and everything. He made me feel special. He says he loves me, and I really like him a lot."

"Russ! What are you doing seeing Mitch all the time then?"

"I told you I'm not old enough to settle down with just one person. My parents fell in love when they were young, and that's great for them, but I'm not like that. I'm not going to say I'm in love when I'm not."

"You're having sex with both of them?" I ask, totally incredulous.

"You don't have to act that shocked," she says. "I like Mitch and Russ. It's not like I just jumped into sex with them both just like that. I was having sex with Russ almost a month before Mitch got anywhere close to that. Now, I'm just comfortable being with both guys. That's not so bad."

"And you used to be the shy one. You wouldn't even talk to guys. I can't believe you're doing that."

"It's not such a big deal. I was honest with both boys. Russ tries to understand, but Mitch is always giving me hassles about it. He can't understand why I would want anybody except him."

"Seems like it would be around school," I say. "You know how everybody talks about each other."

"If a guy respects you, he's not going to gossip about you. Only a jerk would put his business out."

"What do your parents think about you and Russ and Mitch?"

"What can they think? Suzy says if I'm mature enough to have sex, then I can make my own decisions. Tom always gives them the evil eye. He would do any guy I dated like that."

"You're going to have to make up your mind

pretty soon," I tell her. "You can't keep both of them on the string forever."

"Why should I have to decide? If I like two guys and they both treat me right, why should I have to pick between them?"

"I guess it's your business. But I can't imagine having sex with two guys. The way I feel now, I would be happy not to have sex again. It wasn't such a big deal."

"I bet if you're with Mark, it would be good because you really love him. Ricky was just an idol to you. You never really thought you had a chance with him."

"I guess that's it. I had Ricky way up there, but as soon as I had sex with him, it was like his image got tainted. He wasn't so great anymore. And when it was happening, I kept picturing Mark. That was the only time when it was even good. Ricky made me feel like he was just after his own satisfaction."

"Ricky is just a pig. He wants all he can get, and he doesn't worry about if the girl gets anything out of it."

"The only thing he was worried about was whether I came. I was just lying there like a broken doll, and he could see I wasn't getting anything out of it, but he still asked. If we have sex again, I'm just going to lie and get it over with."

"I think you should give Mark a chance."

"He's not going to want me now. Anyway, we got into a fight during Math class. He let me know he doesn't care anything about me. That's one of the reasons I went along with Ricky. At least he wants me."

"You probably won't even see Ricky anymore. The only girl he sees all the time is Cathy. He just hits and runs with the other girls."

"It's funny, but I don't even care anymore. I'm going to go out and have fun and forget all about Ricky Flecher."

At least one good thing has come out of this whole thing. I don't have to have that talk with my parents anymore. I think I know everything about sex. You just lie there, let him do what he wants, and wait for the guy to get finished. The trouble with Ricky is that he doesn't get tired that easily and he doesn't need any motivation.

CHAPTER 17

I've had a few more dates with Ricky. I don't know why he even bothers to take me to the movies or anything. I can tell that he's just itching to get to Huffington Beach. Sex is all he's after anyway. I try not to worry about it. I know I'm not in love with Ricky, and I don't care how he feels about me.

Anyway, since I've been seeing Ricky, I've had a lot of dates with other top guys. I go, but if they're expecting me to put out, they're wrong. Ricky is enough. I bet he's been telling them he scores or something. It's expected anyway. You don't date a guy like Ricky without giving up something.

At least I've gotten something in return. I'm popular. Gale has even started talking to me again. It's like now I have something to offer. I don't let her get to me. I don't trust her any more than I do those other phonies. I have so many friends that I couldn't count them all, and everyone seems to know me now. I can't walk down the hall at Central without getting a "Hi" from some stranger. I went from being almost invisible to one of the most popular girls at school.

That's all I ever wanted, but the funny thing is that I can't handle it. Jody didn't even want to be accepted, and she takes it in her stride. She's Captain of the Girls' Varsity Basketball team, and everybody credits Jody for the team winning so much. Those feats are exceptional because usually, Central's teams suck. Everybody cares so much about how Jody has completely turned things around for the team, so she's influential around the school, and everybody treats her like she's such a top girl. Jody just shrugs it off, and she doesn't let everybody's behavior affect her. She's always complaining about the kids at school being such phonies. I wish I could just do that and not care so much about everyone liking me. Still, I'm always worrying about whether a person is really interested in me or whether they're just out to improve their own popularity. It makes me be on my guard more. I need to watch everything that I do and what I say.

The kids at school have really started treating me differently. They act like I'm not the same old person I used to be. I haven't changed that much. Sure, I'm in the spotlight now, but it hasn't made me a completely different person. I still think the same way I used to, and I'm as unsure about things as ever. Mostly, I'm trying to find my place at school. I don't want people to like me just because I'm dating Ricky. I want people to like me for myself.

Is that too much to ask for? I've always wanted a lot of friends, and I wanted to belong, but I didn't want people to pretend that I’m accepted by them. I still feel like I don't fit in. Maybe if I had worked hard at being so popular, I would feel differently. But it happened so fast, and I didn't have anything to do with it.

The person I wanted to impress most was Diane. I thought she would think I was important and maybe want to be my friend. That's all I ever wanted. I've tried all kinds of things to get her to accept me, and nothing works. She doesn't even care about me being in the “in” group. She acts like they're just regular kids.

Diane's about the only one. Everybody else seems to look up to me because I've started hanging out with Ricky's group. I have to say I'm a part of the group because Ricky has been bringing me around, and they seem to accept me. Even Cathy and that's strange. It's like she's stepping aside and welcoming the new girl.

I don't understand her. She has all the confidence in the world, and there are plenty of guys who would probably date her, but she's sticking with Ricky and taking shit like that off him. Cathy is not bad looking. She probably could be called pretty, and she's really sophisticated. She acts a lot older than she is, and Cathy thinks she's totally chic.

I don't feel sorry for Cathy because she's always trying to put me down. She's reliable about that. She likes talking about everybody. She's the one who put out that Slam List, describing everyone in school and giving her opinion of who belonged under what label. There were the Creeps, the Freaks, the Boozers, the Dope-heads, the Nerds, the Dorks, the Nobodies, the Total Losers, the Wannabes, the Pure Posers, and at the top she put the "in" group. Everyone pretended not to notice it, but I bet everyone saw it. There was even a special Assembly about it, and Mr. Reese tried to calm all the fuss down.

A lot of people didn't like Cathy after that happened. It's one thing to look down your nose on practically everyone at school, but when you make a Slam List like that, you're asking for trouble. I bet she's about the most hated person at school. I guess that's why nobody cares how Ricky treats her. She deserves it. She deserves even worse.

I guess I should feel guilty about seeing Ricky. I don't. If she can't hang onto her boyfriend, it's her problem. I'm going to keep on seeing him for as long as he wants me, and she can take it any way she pleases. If she has something to say, she can just say it to Ricky, but so far, she hasn't caused any trouble. In the morning, I sit at the table with everyone. All she does is roll her eyes at me.

I just smile back, and I act as if I belong. The situation really makes me feel strange. The first time Ricky brought me around, I was so uncomfortable, and I could see everyone staring at me. It was like I was stepping in where I didn't belong, and they didn't know how to take me. And the regular kids treated me differently. Now, I'm used to being around the group, and it's like I'm suddenly somebody special. A few weeks ago, I was a total nobody, but now it's like I'm a special somebody.

I'm in the "in" group, and that's supposed to be the highest you can get at Central. I used to think the group was always doing something wild and that they had so much fun, but they really don't do much of anything. Except maybe talk about the other kids.

They all have better-than-everyone-else attitudes. I thought it was just Cathy, but you can tell by the way they talk that they all feel that way. I don't feel like I'm more significant than I am. Sometimes, it's hard making me feel like I'm a part of things, so I do a lot of pretending. I act like I'm so relaxed and at ease, but I don't really feel that way.

I have nothing in common with the others in the group. Janice is a Honey Bear, Cathy models sometimes, the guys are all jocks, and all of them are rich. My father makes a decent amount of money, but we're not even comfortable. We are forced to do without a lot of things, and Dad doesn't like spending anything on me.

I can tell that they get anything they want without any hassles. I guess I would be stuck-up too if I got everything my way, and I didn't have to worry about nothing except how to spend my big allowance. They take what they get for granted. I bet if they had to live life like me the way they deserve and they had to beg for something sometimes, it would cut them down to size. Talk about a group with swelled heads.

There are eight others in the group. Of course, Ricky and Cathy, Laurie McDonalds and Doug Wright, Sherry Phillips and David Peters, Mike Hodges, and Janice Williams. Mike and Janice were going together, but her mother thinks Janice is too young to just be seeing one guy, so they date other people. They still get together when we want to do something as a group, so everything would be okay if it wasn't for Cathy. When I'm around, she can either get left at home or find herself another date. She makes things uncomfortable by dragging along, and she never goes out with anybody else.

I see her watching Ricky and me the whole time. She must really love the guy. I think she's crazy to take that kind of shit. I haven't talked to Ricky about them. I figure it's none of my business, and he hasn't said anything about the guys I date. But I wonder what he's thinking about to bring me around his girlfriend and introduce me to their friends.

Maybe he has all the confidence in the world, and he doesn't care what other people think. I know the guys have talked to him about it. Janice is really close to Cathy, and I bet she has had Mike try to work on Ricky. I know I'll never get along with either one of them. Janice is friendly enough, but I know she doesn't like me. She's barely civil. Cathy doesn't speak to me unless the bitch needs to. Then she talks to me like I need to have the dumbest words or else I won't understand.

Sherry acts decently to me. She always tries to include me in the conversation, and she doesn't talk down to me. We have a lot of parties at her house. Her mother has been married three times, and she's either out on a date with a prospect for marriage number four or else she's upstairs, and she doesn't want to be disturbed. I could never have a party the way Sherry has. The sky is the limit. The neighbors don't even complain. I guess they're used to it.

Maybe I'll never really fit in with the group. Sometimes, I feel like I don't belong. I've talked about it with Ricky, and he tells me not to worry about it, but it's not as easy as that. I would feel better if we were sneaking around. With everything out in the open, I wonder what people think about me. I remember that there was a time when I did what I wanted, and I didn't care what everyone thought. Now, it seems like I think about it all the time.

CHAPTER 18

Most of the kids are waiting on a showdown between Cathy and me. So far, she hasn't tried anything. She just smiles at Ricky, and she keeps giving me shitty looks. Maybe she's scared to talk to Ricky about it. I wouldn't take that kind of shit from a guy. Not even Ricky Flecher. Everyone is talking about how much I see Ricky. Usually, he hits and runs, but this time he is staying around. Gale asked what I had that keeps him coming back for more.

I would like to know the answer to that question too. It can't be sex. Ricky could get that from anyone. Besides, I'm not that good. I just let him have his way. Sometimes, I think about it all, and it doesn't make any sense. Ricky can have any top girl at school he wants, and he's been dating me. I see him about three times a week, and sometimes we even go out on weekends. Last Saturday, he took me to a party, and it was like everything was all right. Nobody looked surprised that he wasn't with Cathy. It's like everyone has accepted the fact that I'm with him a lot of the time, and it's nothing.

Sometimes, Ricky calls my house just to talk. That's how Mom and Dad found out I was seeing him. You would have thought I did something big - not only date a guy. Dad knows his father, and he thought it was great that Ricky finds me compelling enough to date. He let me have a later curfew, and he never says anything when I'm late. It's like Dad thinks if I'm out with Ricky that everything is okay. I bet he would die if he knew we spent most of our time having sex. All he cares about is that Ricky's father has a lot of money, and Ricky's a football player. Football and money are the most important things to him.

Mom just told me to be careful. Still no talk about the facts of life, but a warning. I felt like telling her I'm on The Pill just to see her reaction. Mom couldn't take the time to teach me about sex, but she just assumes that I'm doing something. It is so unfair, and she makes me so mad. I will never have the kind of closeness with my mother that I want. I know I'm so confused. Mom made me that way by never telling me anything I need to know about life or how to deal with all this shit. I still have so many things I want to talk over with her, but I don't even bother. I figure if she wanted me to know the answers, she would have told me something by now.

Diane comes into the room, and she ignores me as usual. She changes into an old pair of jeans, and she pulls on a yellow Central Bears sweatshirt. She catches me staring at her, and I turn away. I wish I could talk to my sister. What's the use of having one if you need to watch everything you say so that you won't get hurt? I might as well be an only child. I wouldn't know the difference.

"Angel, you really should be more careful," she says. "I found your birth control pills. What if Mom had found them?"

"What were you doing in my drawer?" I demand. "You don't want me bothering your stuff."

"I needed to borrow a bra," she explains. "I didn't have one clean."

"You could have asked."

"You weren't here. I didn't hurt anything, and I wasn't snooping."

"Well, I found your birth control pills a long time ago, so you're not too careful either."

"You had to be snooping."

"I was looking for something else."

"Oh sure, and you expected to find it under my bed."

"This is my room too."

"Just leave my stuff alone. I don't need you watching everything I do and reporting it to Mom and Dad."

"You know I don't tell them anything."

"You better not. I don't need Mom and Dad on my case about anything else." She looks at me. "How did you get those pills anyway? I'm seventeen, and I had a hard time getting mine."

"That's my secret."

"I guess this means what everyone is saying is true," she says. "You're having sex with Ricky Flecher."

"At least he's better than some zit face jerk who doesn't know what he's doing. He's nice to me, and he treats me right."

"Who are you kidding? He's still going steady with Cathy Rankin. He doesn't care anything about you."

"You sound jealous. You're just mad because I have somebody like Ricky."

"I could have had Ricky Flecher a long time ago if I wanted him. He's not my type. I don't want anybody who has to sneak around to be with me."

"Ricky isn't sneaking around. Everybody knows about us. He takes me out all the time, and he brings me around his friends."

"That just shows how dumb you are. Nobody with any sense would have the nerve to come in some girl's face with her boyfriend."

"She's the one who's taking it. If Ricky wants to treat her that way, it's her problem."

"You're too inexperienced to have a guy like Ricky for your first boyfriend."

"I can handle myself. I know what I'm doing. Ricky Flecher or nobody else is going to get the best of me."

"Suit yourself. You think you can handle Ricky. You wouldn't be the first. That guy goes through girls like he has a quota to fill, and he leaves them crying their eyes out over him."

"I'm not crying over any guy," I assure her. "There is always another one out there."

"You've had your warning. If you want to keep on with Ricky, it's your business. I say he's going to use you like he uses everybody else."

"I'm not worried about it."

Diane goes on downstairs. She finally gives me some of her time, and it needs to be a downer. I don't need her giving me that kind of talk. I know what I'm doing. Ricky is getting really interested in me, and I'm going to work on him. I'm going to get him so hooked on me that he'll dump Cathy and he'll let me take her place.

CHAPTER 19

After the movies, Ricky drives to Huffington Beach. I expect things to go like they always do. He takes the blanket out of the trunk, and we start walking along. He has his arm around me, and I put my arm around him. I watch the water. That way, I don't have to think about anything.

"We're good together, aren't we, Angel?"

I think he's talking about sex. "I guess so."

"I've never felt about any girl the way I feel about you. I can't get you out of my mind."

"You must've don't give me too much thought. You date plenty of other girls, and you're still going steady with Cathy."

"I broke things off with Cathy last night."

"Oh."

"I want us to give it a shot." He pauses. "I've never dated a girl like you before."

"What do you mean by that?"

"I'm not trying to put you down. You're different. You don't let things get you all upset. You see me with other girls, and it doesn't even bother you. Most girls would get jealous and start some trouble."

"You can do what you want. I can't tell you who to see. We're both free. I date other guys."

"I don't want you to see anybody else anymore. I want you all to myself."

"I'm not having sex with anybody else. You know that, don't you?"

"I wasn't sure."

"I'm not like that. I only want one guy at a time."

"Do you like it?"

"Like what?"

"You know, being with me."

"I've never had sex with anybody else. I guess I like it."

"You really turn me on. That's why I kept coming back for more. I've never seen any girl as much as I see you without going steady with her."

"Is that supposed to make me feel special?"

"Why is it so hard for you to take a compliment? You act like you're on your guard."

"I have to watch myself."

"You can trust me. You should know that by now. I haven't treated you bad. I take you out, and I try to give you a good time. If I just wanted sex, I wouldn't bother."

"I'm not used to guys like you, Ricky. All kinds of girls are after you, and you pick me. It makes me wonder why."

"I like you, Angel. I did since the start. I could tell you dug me too, and you weren't too afraid to show it. I remember that night at Cassidy's. I thought I could have what I wanted if I asked, but I didn't want things to be like that. I wanted it to be more."

Ricky stops near the pier, and he spreads the blanket. I guess he didn't feel like climbing all those rocks. Ricky pulls me down to him, and we lie on the cover. I expect him to try something, but he doesn't. I look up at the stars. It seems somehow different this time. I don't know why Ricky is telling me all this stuff. He acted cool the other times, and we hardly talked about anything.

"It's nice here. When it gets colder, we're going to have to find some other place, though."

"Hmmm."

"I've never brought any other girl here. It's like this is our place."

"I bet a lot of couples come here to make out."

"I've never seen anybody. I used to come here a

lot when I was a little kid. My father was so busy with work, and my mother had her Charities, so they never had much time for me. I used to ride my bike all the way over here and go swimming. Now, I just go driving."

"I'm not close to my parents, either."

"It's not like that. My parents are there for me when I really need them - it's just that I wanted more. I used to think about going fishing with my dad, but we never did stuff like that. I've always had everything I wanted, but I never had their time, and that's all I ever really wanted. Maybe it would be different if I wasn't an only child. I would have somebody to talk to."

"I have a sister, and it doesn't mean I have someone to talk to."

"Diane is one weird chick. Nobody knows where she's coming from. She floats along in a world of her own."

"Most guys like her."

"She's okay, I guess, but she's not my type."

"I thought all girls were your type."

"I'm choosy when it comes to the girl I really want to be with. I don't want anybody who's always giving me hassles. That's what I like about you. You take things easy."

"Why don't you give me a chance then?"

"That's what I've been trying to tell you. I want

to go steady with you."

"Do you mean that?"

"Yeah, I think we should give it a try."

I throw my arms around him, and I give him a passionate kiss. I've never shown him that much affection before, and he seems to like it. I expect things to go fast, but Ricky can be thoughtful when he wants to. It is the best time yet. I guess when I'm having sex because I want to; it's different than when I'm doing it to make him happy. Maybe it helps to know he feels something for me. I don't love him, but I think I'm beginning to feel something for Ricky.

CHAPTER 20

I go over to Jody's house because I'm so upset. I saw Ricky with another girl, and it really hurt me. I'm not in love with him, but I still can't watch him with someone else without it affecting me. I guess it's just ego or something. We haven't even been going steady for over a month. I know it was all words to him. I bet he never meant to be faithful.

Ricky had me believing all that shit. That he really cared about me, and I'm the first girl he really felt something about. I should have my head examined for even buying that shit. I knew how he was. I don't know why I expected him to change. I guess it was because he sounded so sincere, and I thought I was seeing another side of him.

Suzy opens the door for me, and she tells me that Jody is upstairs in her room. I go and find Jody lying on her bed with her headphones on. I tap her on the shoulder, and she flips over. Jody takes off her headphones, and she sits up in bed. I don't sit down because I can't even stand still. I have so much energy and nowhere to put it.

"You look like you could kill somebody."

"Thanks. I was just telling myself how much I need Jody to tell me that I look like I could kill somebody."

"What's eating you?"

"Ricky wasn't around to drive me home. I went over to Pop Tofflers, and I saw him snuggled up with this dizzy redhead."

"Don't take it so hard."

"That's easy for you to say. I'm only lucky that I was able to get out the door before Ricky saw me."

"I'm surprised you didn't stand up to him," she says.

"I wouldn't want him to know I cared," I say. "He promised that he wouldn't see other girls."

"Did you really expect him to change? You know how Ricky is when it comes to girls. He cheated on Cathy with you, so it's only natural that he'll keep on cheating."

"I don't want to hear that," I say. "I didn't come over here for you to tell me how hopeless it is."

"What do you want me to say?"

"I don't know." I pause. "I'm not stupid like Cathy, though. He's not going to treat me like that."

"What can you do to stop him?" she asks. "Ricky can do whatever he wants, and there's nothing you can do about it."

"For one thing, I'm going to hold out on him. If he wants to be with another girl so bad, let her satisfy his needs."

"Ricky isn't going to go for that."

"There isn't anything he can do about it. I should play out on him. Two can play at his game."

"You wouldn't hurt anybody except yourself," she lectures.

"Why can't you just be my friend?" I demand. "Why do you have to be my conscience?"

"I am your friend. What do you expect me to say?" she asks. "Go out and screw another guy, so Ricky will be jealous?"

"It seems to be working for you," I say. "You have Russ and Mitch fighting each other over you."

"You know I'm not trying to make them jealous of each other. I like Mitch and Russ. It doesn't compare to what you're about to do."

"At least I'm not so mixed up that I can't decide which guy I want."

"Look at yourself," she retorts. "You're supposed to be in love with Mark, but you're having sex with Ricky."

“I happen to go steady with Ricky,” I inform her. “Mark doesn't mean anything to me anymore.”

“Sure, he doesn't,” she says. “That's why you're always staring at him as if you want him so bad.”

“Looking is nothing,” I say. “You're having sex with two guys at the same time.”

“Well, neither one of them is treating me like dirt, so I don’t have to worry about getting hurt.”

“Ricky is not hurting me.”

“Sure, he's not. That's why you're so upset about this other girl because you can take it. Ricky knows just how to get to you. He knows you want everything you don't have. He shows up with another girl, and you run to him with open arms.”

“You act as if you know me so well.”

“I know you like a book. You pretend to be so tough, and you mess with people who are scared that you will kick their ass. But you let Ricky get away with everything. Around everyone else, you keep your guard up, and it's like nothing gets to you. But you leave yourself open for Ricky to get inside and dog you out.”

“That's stupid,” I say. “I don't leave myself open for Ricky to abuse me. I treat Ricky the same way as everybody else.”

“I'm just trying to tell you something for your own good. You're always saying you're a taker, but you're nothing compared to Ricky. He's going to keep on taking until there's nothing left. What are you going to do when he's through using you? Then, he has decided that there's somebody better out there?"

"He's not using me. I'm not that stupid. Ricky is helping me get in with the important people at school. He's not taking anything from me - he's mostly giving. Besides, I can walk away any time I want."

"I just bet you can. Ricky isn't going to let you dump him. He'll be the one who calls it quits, and you'll be the one with the broken heart. I would try to get out now before he really starts taking over."

"I can handle Ricky."

"You never do anything smart. You always take the hard route. You wouldn't have even gotten into this mess if you hadn't been so anxious to take your clothes off."

"Look who's talking," I say. "You're not exactly Ms. Innocent."

"At least it didn't happen at the beach, and at least I saw Russ the next day," she says. "He didn't tell me he was seeing somebody else the next night. All you meant to Ricky was another piece of ass."

"At least I'm not a bastard," I say proudly. "My parents loved each other enough to get married."

"My parents love each other too, and I know they love me. Your parents don't give a damn about you. I have my head on straight, and I'm not a boozer."

"I'm not a boozer!"

"Sure, you're not. That's why you need to drink every day. You always try to act like it's just something you like to do, and it's no big thing, but I know how far it's gotten. I've seen that thermos in your locker, and I'm not dumb. Your ass can't even get through the school day without a pick-me-up."

"Well, I'm not a big baby like you. You're too scared to try anything because you're worried your parents will get mad and leave you. You're too scared to even sleep at my house because you think they'll be gone when you get back home."

"I didn't tell you that for you to throw it back in my face."

"Did I hit a nerve? Before you try to put me down about drinking, you should look at your own self. You're so hung up on being just like Suzy that you started screwing around at fifteen because that's when she started having sex with Tom. Still, you're never really going to be like her because you can't make your skin turn black. You're always putting yourself on a pedestal when you compare yourself to me, but let me tell you something, I'd ten times rather be like me than as screwed up as you are."

"You deserve everything Ricky does to you. You think you're so damn bad, but you won't stand up to him. Talk to him about the shit he does to you and see won't he knock your ass out."

"Are you waiting for him to fight your battles for you?" I sneer. "I don't see you trying to get bad."

"I'm not scared of you."

"You should be. I'm not going to back down this time. You think you're so special, but I can knock you back down where you belong."

"Get out of my room! I hate you, and I don't care if I ever see you again! You can go to Hell for all I care!"

"You'll need me before I need you," I say as I head out the door. "Just remember that."

"Oh yeah? We'll just see about that. You're going to come begging for me when you need a real friend, and I'm not going to be there for you anymore. You think you're so important because you have all those phonies smiling in your face and you try to treat me like trash. Well, I'm not going to take it anymore, because I've had enough of your shit and I'm through being a doormat for you. Don't hold your breath waiting for me to apologize this time, because as far as I'm concerned, we've said everything we have to say to each other."

Downstairs, Tom and Suzy are watching TV, but I just walk past them without saying anything. I know they heard Jody and me fighting, but they don't try to confront me about it. I don't care what they think, and I don't care about Jody. Maybe it's good that we broke up our friendship. She always did think she was better than me. I don't need a friend like that. I'd rather be alone.

CHAPTER 21

I have been going steady with Ricky for three months. I should be happy, but I'm miserable. We do a lot of things with his group, and that's better than being alone with him, but I'm tired of the whole thing. I need to be up all the time, and sometimes it's hard. I feel like I can never show my real emotions or act the way I really am. I don't want to be a phony, but nobody cares about the real me. The only identity I have is being Ricky's girl. Nobody cares about anything else about me, because that is all that is important as far as they are concerned.

I need to stay on my guard all the time. I watch what I say around Ricky's friends. They all seem so assured of themselves, and I feel like I'm not good enough for them. They make me feel like I need to do shit to measure up. Being Ricky's girl is not enough for them. That's what got me in, but now I need to prove myself. I still don't feel comfortable around them.

There's this table in the cafeteria, and nobody

sits at it except the "in" group. We spend every morning there, and we hold court because all the other kids are being judged all the time. A lot of kids look over at us, and I know they're envious. The funny thing is, we're not doing anything except talking about the unpopular kids. Cathy Rankin is the worst. Sometimes, it sounds like she hates anybody who's not as affluent as she is.

Mostly, I don't say anything except when someone brings up my silence. I don't like games. What if somebody isn't in with the popular kids? That doesn't give us any reason to talk about them. And Cathy is always talking about Jody. We're not friends anymore, but I still get offended. For some reason, Cathy hates Jody's guts, and she doesn't keep quiet about it.

By now, everybody knows about Jody's parents. Not about them living together, but that they're a mixed couple. It doesn't matter to Cathy that Jody has about as much money as she does. She can't get over the fact that Jody's not totally white. Cathy can make some crude jokes about it. She's also always putting Russ and Mitch down about having anything to do with Jody. Sheila Haskle is dating Lenny Michaels now, but nobody gives her a hassle about it.

Cathy really gets on my nerves sometimes. She had the gall to say, "Don't worry, Angel. You're not going to be around that long. Nobody is. Besides, you're not even in our class." I may be low-life as far as she's concerned, but I let her know that I have more class in my little finger than she has in her entire body.

I may be acting like a slut with Ricky, but at least it's not rumored about me that I have sex with every guy that I date.

I know Cathy's just trying to get Ricky back. She's always flirting with Ricky and teasing him about the old times. Cathy asks stupid questions, and he always gives a cute reply to her. She makes me so mad when she does that. I know what a worm Cathy is, and the bitch will just love to wiggle her way into our relationship. Whenever she does something like that, I hold on more to Ricky. I don't like anybody messing around with something I've got. Even if I don't love Ricky, that doesn't mean I want some other girl taking my place. Especially if it is his ex-girlfriend.

Shana Black is always coming into my face with the latest Cathy's done to capture his attention. I know she is a friend of Cathy's, and she only does that so she can go back to report my reaction to Cathy, so I always act like it doesn't bother me. But it really burns me up. I hate being around Cathy.

Every time we go out, I know she is going to be along. There are enough couples to go around, but Cathy is left out. She can either get a date or be the fifth wheel. Mostly, she goes alone, and she spends the entire evening making time with Ricky. I sit there feeling like a dummy, and I wonder why I put up with that kind of shit.

Ricky says that Cathy doesn't mean anything to him. That they've known each other all their lives and their parents are best friends, so he needs to talk to her. I know his parents like Cathy more than they like me, and they would be happy if Ricky took back up with her. She's a snob and everything, but she's more the type of girl that they would like for their son.

I've only met his parents once. Ricky took me around one day, and he introduced me to them. They were polite, but I felt out of place. I bet they knew that I was from the wrong part of town and that I didn't have a lot of money. I guess they said something to him about it because he hasn't bothered to take me home with him again. Not that I would like to go through that whole scene another time and be put on the spot like that.

Sometimes, I think there's something seriously wrong with Ricky. Like the way he treats me. He likes having sex with me, but he's started getting kinky. I go along with him, but not when I'm sober. He doesn't force me to do anything I don't want to, but he can be persuasive. He gets to telling me about all he's done for me and talking about how I owe him something. I don't need him to be laying all that shit on me, so I just go along with him.

I would be ashamed if somebody like Jody found out. What she thinks about me still matters to me. The gossip about me at school is heavy, but it only scratches the surface. I'm sure Ricky's the one who runs his mouth. I don't say anything about my sex life. Some girls joke about their sexual experience, and they act like they don't care what people think. I'm not like that. I don't care about not being a virgin, but my reputation means a lot to me.

That's why I don't like carrying on in front of everyone. Ricky loves to make out around his friends, and he gets pretty carried away. When I push his hands away, he acts like I've done something to hurt him. I just don't like to be on display. He feels like I'm rejecting him or something crazy like that.

“You act like you don't want me touching you,” he complains.

“It's not that.”

"What is it, then?”

“I don't like making out in front of everybody.”

“You act like you're ashamed or something.”

“Why do we have to let the world know what we do?”

“If you cared about me, you wouldn't mind if people saw you showing me.”

“I'm not out to get some attention that way,” I say. “Haven't I shown you yet how I feel about you?”

“Everybody else is doing the same thing, and nobody worries about it. I don't know why you're trying to act like you’re so shy about sex.”

“Whatever I say, you're not going to understand. You never try to understand what I'm trying to say.”

“Because you never make any sense. You're my

girl. Everybody knows we're messing around. Why should we try to hide anything?"

I know there's no use explaining things to Ricky. He gets a kick out of showing his friends what we do. It doesn't matter if I'm embarrassed or not in the mood. We fight about it all the time, but I'm not going to give in about that. I have no desire to prove all the gossip right and show everyone what a slut I can be. Ricky stays mad about it, but he knows when not to push me because I can be a real bitch sometimes, and he's learned what that's like. He can do what he likes when we're alone, but the rest of the time, I'm off-limits, and he just needs to accept that and quit pressuring me all the time. Sometimes, I think he just wants me for one thing.

CHAPTER 22

Things have been going pretty much the same. It's gotten so that everything is routine to me. I thought I would be so excited about going to those parties and being in the "in" group that I'd never come down. But the excitement didn't even last that long. I'm just used to the way the other kids treat me. It hasn't gone to my head, but I just take it as it comes.

The other kids do weird things like give me answers like I'm the dumbest person in class or ask me answers like I'm this big brain. I'm no dummy, and I'm not too smart either, so I wish they would stop. Girls who always ignored me, now find me so interesting that I'm almost always late for class because I get held up talking. What a bunch of phonies. I wish someone would just like me for myself and forget that I'm Ricky's girl.

Jody really understood how I felt about things, but we haven't made up yet. I know I said some hurtful things to her, and she probably won't forget them.

I wish I could just call her and say I'm sorry, but she definitely wouldn't forgive me. I don't know what gets into me. Jody was the best friend I ever had, and I had to ruin everything. Maybe I just don't want anybody to get close to me. She knew what a confused girl I was inside, and she got to befriend the person I hide from everyone else, and she liked me anyway. Now, I am back to pretending and hiding my real feelings.

I feel like nobody even likes me and they just seek my opinion, because they think it's the thing to do. After all, I'm so popular, and they never care what I really think. It's like I just hear a bunch of shit that people think I want to hear, and they could care less about me. I have so many damn friends, but I feel lonely most of the time, and I know I can't depend on anybody for support. I feel like everyone changed so much, and I'm still the same mixed-up person I was, and I have a lot of fears, but nobody wants to go beyond the surface and find the real me. I've always kept so many things to myself, but I would like for someone to take the time to even find out about the parts of me that I've never left exposed. I know nobody wants to go that deep, and I will never have a friend like Jody again because true friendship really means something. Still, I'm left with people hanging on just because it's the thing to do, and they would turn on me at the slightest chance.

I feel like I will never be an individual again, and people only think of me as Ricky's girl, and that's my only identity. They felt like I was nobody before him, and after him, I will just be a loser again. I remember how things were before I got hooked up with Ricky, and sometimes that time doesn't seem as bad as I always made it seem. At least, I was happy sometimes. Now, I'm forever pretending, and my whole life is an act. Maybe I am just the biggest phony of all, and the real Angel Moore won't ever have a chance to be exposed again. I hate how I am now so much, but I think about how things used to be, and I'm not all anxious to go back to that either, so I don't know why I'm even complaining. I should be so grateful for having Ricky for my boyfriend and having him doing so much for my popularity. Then knowing I have a secure place at school. I just get so sick of him, and I hate every part of our relationship.

Ricky does a lot of things to get on my nerves, but I just smile, and I act like it doesn't even bother me. Sometimes, I feel like telling him where he can go, but I never talk back to him. Like when I see Ricky with other girls, I feel like asking him where he gets off, and I want to make a big scene. But I just take it like a dummy. I never thought I would ever put myself into this kind of position with a guy. Losing all my confidence and spending half my time convincing him he's so important. Ricky makes me so sick, and I hate the sight of him, but nobody would ever suspect it by the show I put on. Being the perfect little girlfriend and being by his side when he needs me there to make an appearance.

I have always been so laid back and in control,

but Ricky knows how to throw me off balance. He wants to tell me what to do and how to do it. If I try to do things on my own, Ricky acts like I need to hear his mouth. He's fine whenever I go along doing everything he says, but if I try to think for myself, he gets mad. Sometimes, I think Ricky just likes to boss me around and control every part of my life. He makes me feel like I'm too stupid to do anything on my own.

Maybe it makes him feel important to be able to control me. He's always saying this and that about being stronger and smarter than me. I'm a 5"2, 113 lb. Girl, so who expects me to be able to handle a 6"1, 190 lb. Football player? Of course, he can slap me around and stuff without me being able to hurt him. And I never claimed to have a genius IQ. Maybe if I was a senior too, I would be as smart as he claims to be. Sometimes, I feel that I really am stupid, or I know I wouldn't put up with all his shit. He likes hitting me at school, and our fights are a daily occurrence. I never talk to anybody about it, and I don't know how he can do me like that, but around other people is the only time he treats me that way. I think it's his way of making people think he's in control because I can't think of any other reason that he does it. I feel bad most of the time, and I know the most significant part of me is just disappearing. I hate the person Ricky is making me become, and I can't even remember how I used to be.

"Shut up" is his favorite expression. Whenever I try to share my opinion when we're with the group, he's always telling me to be quiet. He can talk all he wants, but he expects me to sit by and listen to him like I'm so impressed by his views on the subject. Maybe I don't have the best ideas, and nobody really cares what I think, but I like expressing myself anyway. I feel like all my thoughts and feelings are getting buried deep inside me. I'm only supposed to share his opinions and let him decide everything for me. Ricky tries to tell me how to do every little thing, and I never have the chance to even speak my mind in peace. He can make me so mad sometimes.

The only time I can really be free is at school. Thank God, I don't have any classes with him, and I eat lunch at a different time. When I'm at home, I can't make any plans, because he might call and want to do something. I'm expected to fit my schedule to suit his needs. Ricky goes where he wants, and he does everything he feels like. If I'm not there nursing the phone on the chance he might call, he'll have something to say about it. Whenever Ricky needs somebody to make him feel good or to massage his ego, I'm on demand. But when he's okay, it's like he doesn't need me.

Ricky is always telling me when I mess up, but I'm supposed to take him the way he is. He does more things to make me mad than I do to get on his nerves. Ricky makes excuses for everything his ass does, and even if Ricky sees that I'm not buying it, Ricky'll keep right on lying. People are always telling me some shit about him, and when I confront him about it. He either denies it, or he laughs it off as not being important.

But if I even smile at a guy, he's all over my case. Ricky can flirt with any girl he sees, but I'm supposed to ignore the opposite sex. If I'm caught talking to some guy, I'm supposed to repeat the entire conversation to him. I feel like he's the one out whoring around, and I'm stuck in the house, but he's putting off all his wrong-doing on me. Maybe if he was faithful too, he wouldn't be worrying about me all the time and trying to make me seem so guilty for even having an interest in other guys. I may look, but that's as far as it would ever go. He's so jealous, and he doesn't even have anything to be wary about.

Mark came over to my house yesterday to work on a History project that we're doing together. Ricky shows up, and he starts accusing me of all sorts of things. We were right in the living room, and anybody could see that it was all innocent. But you would've thought we were in my bedroom with the door locked. Instead of causing any trouble, Mark just got his stuff, and he left. Ricky said I had been coming on to Mark, and that's why he was there.

Ricky has never liked the fact that we are friends, and he said I couldn't be around Mark anymore. I told him I could be friends with anyone I like, and he didn't have anything to say about it. Mark is the only real friend I have left. I wasn't going to let him ruin things. Ricky's still ticked off about it, but that's just too bad. I don't tell him who to be friends with.

Sometimes, he makes me so mad I could scream!

CHAPTER 23

Sherry invites me to spend the night with her on Friday. Her mother is going to be gone for the weekend, and she didn't want to stay by herself. Sherry is the only one of Ricky's friends who has treated me like I'm somebody besides Ricky's girl, and Sherry talks to me like I'm a person. Maybe she is as rich and as big of a snob as the other members of the "in" group. Still, I feel like in some ways she is different, and she just tries to keep up the pretense, because when we're alone sometimes and her guard is down, I feel like she's just like a regular girl with the same fears and stuff as me.

I arrive at Sherry's house around 7:30, and we watch some TV. Sherry fixes us Fuzzy Navels, and I taste my drink. It's sweet, but I drink it. There's a whole pitcher of the stuff, and I guess the two of us are supposed to drink it. I'm used to stronger drinks, and so it doesn't affect me that much. I make another drink, and Sherry switches the station. She has so many channels on her TV, and she just keeps flipping through them. Finally, she just leaves the station on MTV. I'm hoping to see the Youth Gone Wild Music Video, because I love all the guys in Skid Row, and I never get to watch that Music Video at home. Of course, I brought their album like all the other girls at school, and I know how gorgeous the guys look, but it would still be nice to see those guys performing that song for once. I don't get to watch any Cable channels that much since we don't even have Basic Cable. It's good that Sherry is lucky enough to have Premium Cable. Still, she says later we can probably watch a movie on HBO. I keep watching the TV screen at all the exciting Music Videos that are playing. I'm able to pay attention to Sherry too, and we talk to each other some.

"We should have had the guys over," Sherry says suddenly.

"Please. I'm happy to have a break."

"You and Ricky haven't been getting along, have you?" she asks. "Whenever we're together, you seem moody."

"I just need some time by myself, but we're always with the group, or I'm alone with him. I never have any time of my own. Sometimes, I would like to spend an evening all by myself just to do what I really want to do and forget everything else."

"I don't feel that way. I would be happy to have Dave all to myself like that."

"But it's not like that. Ricky dates other girls, but I'm supposed to be faithful. That's not fair."

"You know what a big ego Ricky has," she explains. "Some guys are just like that."

"He doesn't have to take it out on me. Going steady is a two-way street. He shouldn't expect me to stay at home being faithful if he's out screwing around."

"Before I let Dave have sex with me, we had to have some ground rules. If he has me, he shouldn't want anybody else. I made sure he wouldn't see other girls. I don't want to catch anything."

"That's what I'm worried about with Ricky. I'm on The Pill, so I can't get pregnant. But what if he catches some disease? You never know what those bitches have got."

"You should put down the law with Ricky. He doesn't even try to hide it. He's always flirting with other girls."

"I thought I would never let a guy treat me like that. I thought Cathy was crazy when he used to bring me around, and she never said anything. Now, he's doing the same thing to me. At least he hasn't brought any girl around our table."

"I think he really cares about you."

"He sure has a funny way of showing it."

"I mean it. Dave said he talks about you all the

time. Saying how much he loves you, and he said you're the first girl he ever cared about."

"Then why does he need all those other girls?" I ask. "And why can't he tell me that?"

"Maybe he has a hard time with his feelings. It's easier for guys to tell some other guys stuff. And Ricky's used to girls throwing themselves at him. I guess it's just hard for him to say 'no.'"

"It's hard going with a good-looking guy. You always need to look over your shoulder. Chances are some girl's trying to stab you in the back."

"If Ricky didn't feel anything for you, he wouldn't keep seeing you."

"Hmmm."

"Nobody has lasted as long as you. Not even Cathy and they've known each other since they were kids."

"Cathy still wants Ricky. I can tell by the way she's always flirting with him. She makes me so sick sometimes. I feel like smacking that smug smile off her face."

"Cathy is hard to take sometimes," she admits. "She's had things too easy."

"She's such a snob. She thinks everybody is beneath her. She keeps her nose up in the air so much that it ought to get stuck that way. I'll never forget how she put out that Slam List."

"It was only supposed to be a joke."

"I bet Cathy was pretty serious about it. I can see how she looks down on people, and she has more than anybody else to say about the unpopular kids."

"Well, we're supposed to be special. If we let just anybody into our group, where would we be? The unpopular kids look up to us, and we have an image to maintain."

"That doesn't mean we have to put those unpopular kids down," I point out. "It doesn't make us better than them."

"What's wrong with you? We're not doing anything wrong."

"It's not fair. Just because the kids aren't popular, that doesn't mean something is wrong with them. I remember when I was down there looking up. I can't forget how I felt. Besides, I know if I wasn't Ricky's girl, I would still be down there."

Sherry doesn't say anything else. I guess I shouldn't have said anything that would ruin things, but that's how I feel. I don't like how the group talks about the other kids. I hardly ever participate. I haven't forgotten where I came from.

CHAPTER 24

The party is just like all the other parties. There's plenty to drink, and there are few people that aren't in Ricky's crowd. Mostly, everyone is just sitting around and talking.

The stereo is playing, and one couple is dancing in the center of the room. It's Sherry's house, and she has a Rec Room in her basement. Their basement looks better than my living room. All the kids in our group have somewhere in their houses where the kids can go and have fun with their friends.

That's why I feel funny when they get to suggest a place to party. There isn't anywhere in my house that we could go to hang out. Except maybe the living room and my mother would want to hang around us. I would feel stupid if I had a party and she was there. Besides, our house isn't good enough to bring those kids over to. I've seen all their places, and ours is nothing compared to theirs.

Ricky doesn't seem to care that I don't have a lot of money, but I know the rest of his group does. They are so used to getting everything their way and having a lot of things that they look at me funny when I say I can't do anything. When I go shopping with Sherry and the others in the "in" group, they are always spending like crazy, but I need to put stuff in the lay-a-way. I know it's the only chance I'll have to get new things and try to keep up with them. Since my father is so happy that I'm seeing Ricky and he's out to impress the Big Shots in town, it seems like he would want me to have decent clothes and stuff, so I won't embarrass him. But he's just as cheap as ever. I've gotten so that I don't even ask him for an allowance anymore. The begging isn't worth it, and my pride can't take it anymore. Besides, Ricky insists on buying me everything I want.

Ricky talks football to a couple of guys. It seems like since the Season is over and Central wasn't any good that he would get tired of talking about that. Ricky even has a scrapbook filled with clippings of him. Ricky showed it to me, and I had to sit there and listen to his account of what was happening during each picture. I should know something about football by now, but the whole subject bores me.

I go over to the bar. Sherry's mother never measures her booze, so we always have plenty to drink when we come to her house. Ricky brought a case of beer anyway, so I fix myself a drink. The only fun thing about these parties is the liquor. Everything else is always the same. The same people and the same subjects. I used to think I would like being able to go all the time to the hippest parties, but it's not fun anymore being at those parties.

About a half-hour goes by. I see Ricky talking to this girl. He makes me so mad. Ricky's always flirting with other girls, and the bastard can't see anything wrong with that, but I can't even talk to other boys. He gets all jealous, and he wants to fight about it. It's like how Ricky can't understand about me being friends with Mark. He said I had to stop hanging around him. I wouldn't do it, and he got all mad. It's bad enough that Jody isn't around anymore. I'm not going to lose the only real friend I have left.

Ricky whispers something to the girl, and she blushes. Usually, I don't say anything, but I'm getting fed up with all his shit. The bastard is just like that. We walk along to someplace, and he looks at all the pretty girls, and he doesn't try to hide the fact that he's checking them out. But I'm supposed to look straight ahead and not even glance in a guy's direction, or he has something to say about it, and he wants to fight. I'm getting so sick of his shit. I guess the alcohol has given me the courage to confront him in front of everybody because I'm furious that he's acting like that in public and not giving me the proper respect. I don't give a shit who knows it. Everybody can see him hitting on the girl, and he knows I'm right here, but he figures he can get away with anything. Well, we'll just see about that.

"Ricky, if you wanted to be with this stupid bitch, why did you even bother bringing me?" I ask, loud enough for everybody to hear. "I don't care who you try to fuck, but don't do it in my face or you might not like what happens, because I'm getting tired of all your stupid shit and I'm not going to put up with it much longer."

I turn around, and I head towards the door. Outside, I start walking in the direction of my house. It's a long way to go, but I don't think about that. I just want to get out of there, and away from all the people I can't stand. It's not long before I hear somebody running after me. Ricky grabs my arm, and he swings me around.

"Don't ever talk to me like that again around my friends."

"I'll talk to you any way I damn well please," I assure him. "Why did you bother following me? I can take a hint. I know when to get lost."

"You've been drinking again, haven't you?" he asks. "You act like you have to be drunk to even be around me."

"I can't be up all the time. I don't want to feel bad, and I don't have to be unhappy. Besides, if I drink, it's my business. It's not hurting you in any way."

"What's happening to you?" he asks. "You used to be such a fun kid."

"What do you think is happening to me? I can't

do anything the way I want. You tell me who to talk to. What to wear. I don't need anybody to make me over. If I'm so bad, why did you even want me in the first place?"

"I keep asking myself that. I don't even know why I bother with you. I take you out on dates to good places, and I treat you right, and you act like it's not enough. What do I have to do to make you happy?"

"You make me feel like I'm just somebody you like to fuck. I have thoughts and feelings, but you never ask my opinion about anything. You just tell me everything to do and how I should act, and you always treat me like I don't know anything. How do you think that makes me feel?"

"Sometimes, you're a real pain in the ass."

"Then maybe you ought to just stop seeing me."

"I'll tell you when I want to call things to quit. Nobody breaks up with me. When I'm through with you, you'll know it."

I just look at him.

"Come on back to the party. This time you better act right. Do you want my friends to know how stupid you actually are?"

I just follow him back to the party like a dummy. I really start hating Ricky at that moment. Before, he just disgusted me, and I hated the thought of him touching me. But at that moment, I realize I hate Ricky so much that I wish something would happen to him.

Anything to get him away from me. I know Ricky meant what he said. I'll never be free from him until he decides that he doesn't want me anymore, and I'm just stuck with him. I feel like I'm dying inside, and I want to cry so bad. Still, I bury the feeling as deep as I can inside me, and I know I'm going to make sure that nobody is ever going to see my pain.

CHAPTER 25

Things have been going okay for me. For one thing, Ricky hasn't been by for three days. The most important thing is that Mark and Linda broke up. I got so happy when I heard that I almost jumped for joy, but I know it doesn't have anything to do with me. I can't tell Mark my true feelings and have him steal me away from Ricky. In the last couple of months, he's been leaning on me a lot. I guess it's hard breaking up with somebody after all that time - even if you don't love them.

Gale said I should stop leading Mark on. She said that he really likes me and he's going to start expecting something from me. How I wish that was true. I still love Mark as much as ever, and I want to be with him. I haven't been dreaming about that, though. I know Ricky would hang on to me just because another guy would desire me. He doesn't love me, but he doesn't want anybody else to have me either.

"I heard about Mark," Linda says. She blocks my

path. I'm so deep in thought that I don't notice her until she does that. I wonder what her problem is. Hasn't she heard? It's over with. There isn't any use coming in my face. It's not like I caused Mark to dump her ass. Mark hasn't tried to talk to me about their breakup, but from the way she's acting, I can guess who called things off.

"What about him?"

"You stay away from him!"

"Mark and I are just friends," I say. "He calls me sometimes - that's all."

"Isn't Ricky enough for you? You should be too sore from him to even want anybody else's man."

"What I do isn't any of your business," I inform her. "Anyway, Mark isn't your man anymore. If he wants to spend some time with me, it's our business, and there's nothing you can do about it."

"You bitch."

"Call me a bitch one more time, and I'll show you what a bitch can do."

"What's the matter? Everybody knows what a big slut you are. You had to fuck Ricky to get him, and you need to keep fucking your ass off to keep him. I've heard first-hand about some of the shit you do. That's why you're nothing but a big bitch."

I hit her tall ass right in the mouth. Before she has a chance to recover, I start slamming her all over. I want to ruin that pretty face. She thinks she's so special, but when I get through with her, nobody will want to be seen with her. I've been so frustrated for such a long time, and that suppressed anger just wants to explode. She falls on the floor, and I'm all over her. I take a handful of her hair, and I wrap it around my fist. I start slamming her head against the floor. I just don't care anymore. I know I'm just going to kill the bitch, and seeing her bleed just makes me want to hurt her worse.

They need to pull me off her. It takes two teachers to hold me back, and I'm still mad. Linda is all messed up. Both her nose and mouth are bleeding, and her eye looks like it's about to close. Her whole face is all puffy, and it already looks like somebody took a bat to her because her face is covered in bruises and cut up bad. I just wish I had hurt her ass worse and caused some permanent damage. Linda's crying like a baby and her friends hold her. Everybody is gathered around Linda feeling sorry for her. I get a few disgusted looks, and somebody says I should try kicking Ricky's ass like that sometimes, and then maybe he wouldn't kick mine so terribly every day. A few other people have some comments for me too. Fuck them. I don't really care what they have to say. It's not like any of this shit is my fault, and I caused the fight. She should know who not to mess with. She's had it coming for a long time, and she was asking for it.

"You are in so much trouble," Mrs. Lewis tells me. "You'll be lucky if the Police aren't called."

“Well, so what?” I ask. “Do you think that's really going to scare me?”

“That's it.” She grabs my arm. “I'm tired of your attitude.”

The Office is crowded. There are a lot of people waiting to see, our principal, Mr. Reese. I take a seat outside his door, and Mrs. Lewis goes back to her class after she explains the situation to the office secretary, Mrs. Reynolds.. Everybody is staring at me, so I must look awful. That bitch really scratched my face up. At least I don't look as bad as she does. I bet they won't even do anything to her. Honey Bears seem to be somehow above the law.

Whatever they do to me, it'll be worth it, because I finally got her back. Linda's been giving me shittiest looks all year, and I'm sure she's one of the main bitches spreading shit around about me. Let her gossip about this. I know the news of the fight will be all over the school, and Ricky will hear about it. I don't really care what he'll think. Same way with my parents. I know they'll give me a hassle about it. Fuck him and fuck them all.

I hate going into Math class. I know I'll have to face Mark and by now he's heard something. He's already at his desk. I take the seat in front of him. I don't try to say anything. Ms. Bonds isn't in class yet, and everybody is talking. I hear a couple of comments about the fight, but nobody really gives it that much attention. At least, nobody says anything to me about it.

"I'm sorry, Angel," Mark says.

"About what?"

"You know, Linda and everything."

"It's not your fault."

"Linda just can't accept the fact that it's over. The past couple of months, she's fucked every guy out there, and she's acted like the biggest skank she could, but the bitch thought I would just be there waiting to get back with her when she got tired of doing that shit. I didn't want her before Linda acted like such a slut, so I don't know why Linda believes I'm going to want her now. She acts like she's so desperate or something. Linda keeps calling my house and hanging up and leaving love notes in my locker and doing a lot of other dumb shit to get my attention. The bitch just won't give up. She even went and told my parents that we were having sex, and she said I owe her something. Hell, I wasn't the first guy she ever had sex with, and I wasn't the last guy she hooked up with. Now, she's going to pull this crazy shit. I don't know what I'm going to do."

"Don't worry. After today, Linda won't bother me anymore."

"I heard you really fucked her up bad," he says. "She had to go home in an ambulance."

"I should have thrown her down the stairs."

"Linda didn't hurt you, did she?"

"You know me better than that," I say. "All Linda had a chance to do was scratch my face."

"It doesn't look that bad," he says.

"I hope not," I say. "All I need is some permanent scars."

"Will this cause trouble between you and Ricky? You know how he's always on your case about us."

"I don't care what Ricky thinks. Anyway, I haven't seen him for three days."

"You don't act as if you miss him."

"He'll be back. I need a break. You know how he is. Wanting to do something every night."

"You never complained before."

"I'm not complaining now."

"I bet you drive a guy crazy," Mark says. "I wish I could try you out."

I give Mark the finger.

"Is that an offer?"

I don't tell him how much I wish it was an offer. I know he'd be a good lover. Better than Ricky. He hurts me a lot, but he says I like it. I don't. I hate it. I know he just wants me for one thing, but sometimes he tries to rub it in. I need to go home and take a long bath to get myself together. I want to wash away all the evidence.

"I can read your mind."

"What was I thinking then?"

"I'm not telling."

"Chicken."

"I'm not chicken about nothing."

"Then tell me what I was thinking."

"I might get into trouble."

"I'm not bashful."

"I know you're not, Angel Moore," he says. "I bet nothing would embarrass you."

"You would win."

"Let's get serious."

"I thought we were serious."

"You call this serious?"

"Shush," Pam Williams says.

"Shut up, you blimp," I retort.

"Who does she go out with?" Mark asks.

"I don't know anybody who would have her," I say loud enough for Pam to hear.

"She can hear you," Mark whispers.

"I don't care," I say. "I heard you tried to fuck Tanya Mitchell."

"I didn't ask her!"

"That's what you say." I sound like I don't believe him. Mark starts blushing. He has never embarrassed me. When Mark blushes, it starts at his nose and spreads over his whole face. I know he's mad that I was able to embarrass him.

"What's wrong with you?"

"What do you mean?" I ask. "I'm always this way."

"You know, you're moody."

I stop to think about it. I guess facing Ricky is making me more upset than I thought. He saw me in the hall, and he told me he would see me later. The way he sounded, he was shitty, and I know there's going to be a scene. I wish he would just stay away forever and leave me alone.

"You're thinking about Ricky."

"How did you know?"

"I told you I could read your mind."

"You haven't proved it yet."

"Mark, Angel, will you give the class a break?"

It's Ms. Bonds. She's looking stern, but the side of her mouth is twitching. I know she's not mad, but we knock it off. Ms. Bonds gets into enough trouble for her teaching methods and stuff. I turn back to the front of the class, and I'm determined to learn something, but it is so hard to concentrate on my work because all I really want to do is hang out with Mark. We do try to keep quiet in the last twenty- three minutes of class. Every time we look at each other, we either burst out laughing or start talking again. It's a miracle that we're even passing the classes that we have together, because this is how we spend most of our time, and I expect that next year our teachers will split us up.

The bell rings.

Mark walks me to my locker. It's almost lunchtime, and we always eat together. My locker is a mess. There's so much junk, and some of my books fall out. It's like a compact size of my room. I share a locker with another girl. So between the two of us, we've managed to save a lot of stuff over the year. Mark leans against my locker and he watches me.

"Excuse me."

Hilary Miller takes Mark's place. She hands me her English book, and she asks for her History book. I dig it out from under the pile at the bottom of the locker. I finally find my change purse, and I slam the door shut.

"Are you going to Janice Williams's beach party?" Hilary asks.

"I don't know. Ricky hasn't said anything about it."

"Everybody at school is going to be at Huffington

Beach. Janice's father is putting out a lot of money. There's even going to be a band."

"It sounds like fun," I say. "Who are you going with?"

"Who else? Larry never lets me out of his sight."

"Must be nice."

"I'd better run. I have to go all the way to the other side of the building."

Hilary runs off. Mark turns towards me.

"Are you going to that party if Ricky doesn't go?"

"I don't want to go alone."

"I'm going with Russ and Jody," he says. "If you want to go along, call me."

"I'll think about it."

We go to the cafeteria. I do a lot of laughing and joking around. Outside, I'm happy, but inside I feel like crying. I always laugh when I feel like crying. I don't know what's wrong with me. I have everything going for me. I'm doing all the things in high school that I thought would be so much fun, but I'm miserable.

Sometimes, I try to think of Ricky and me positively. Since I'm stuck with him, I try to find ways that I could be happy with him. Sometimes, I imagine us going to Tesselman Park and having a picnic. But nothing like that ever happens. We go to Huffington Beach, and we have sex. The sex is so lousy, and I don't get into it. Only, I lie to get it over with, and I say the right things to keep Ricky happy and stop him from getting mad and causing another one of our fights. When I finally get home, I take a long bath, and sometimes I cry.

When I look in the mirror, I don't seem to like the person I see. Ricky is always putting me down, and I'm beginning to believe him. I think I'm blah. That I don't have much personality or anything else that is important. That's how I feel about myself now. I don't have any confidence in myself anymore. Mostly, I just go along. There's nothing important. I only exist, and it's a rotten existence.

CHAPTER 26

When I get home from school, Mom is all upset, and Dad is even there from work. He starts fussing about the fight I got into with Linda. I guess her parents called Mom, and she got Dad on the phone. He acts like I should have stood there and let Linda beat me up or something.

"What did you expect me to do?" I ask. "Stand there like a dummy and let her beat me up?"

"You didn't have to beat that girl so savagely. We're going to have to pay her medical bills. She had to get stitches to sew up her mouth, and her jaw is broken. Her parents say her face is black and blue, and one of her eyes is swollen shut. How could you be so ruthless?"

"She shouldn't have come in my face starting some stuff. She's just lucky I didn't hurt her a lot worse. If those teachers hadn't pulled me off her, I would have really gotten her."

"You're not even sorry. You nearly put a girl in the hospital, and you're bragging about what you could have done."

"Linda asked for it. What have I got to feel sorry about? If it was the other way around, she wouldn't be sorry about beating me up. Next time, Linda will know who she can mess with and who she should stay away from."

Dad can see that he can't get to me, so he leaves me alone. I know he's only worried about the medical bill. Dad could care less about what we do. I bet if money hadn't been involved, he wouldn't have even said anything to me about it.

Mom makes me put iodine on my cuts. If they were going to get infected, it would have happened by now, but I do what she says. My face isn't as bad as I first thought it was. It'll heal in a day or two.

Diane comes home about an hour later. I'm sitting on my bed. She dumps her books on her desk, and she sits down on her bed. She keeps looking at me, but she doesn't try to say anything. It's funny thinking about Diane being shy about something. She's usually always talking and frank about everything.

"What's wrong, Diane?" I finally ask.

"Nothing really. I heard about your fight. Everybody was talking about it. You really hurt Linda."

"I hope you're not going to give me a lecture too."

"Nope." She pauses. "I guess she really deserved it. I've heard her talking about you, and everyone was saying she started it."

"She thinks I'm after her ex-boyfriend."

"Mark Davis? He's kind of cute. He wasn't Linda's speed, though. She needs somebody who loves to party and likes to be in with the crowd. Mark isn't like that."

"How do you know so much about Mark?"

"He's a friend of Keith's. We've talked some. He really loves you, and I think you ought to give him a chance. He's ten times better than that jerk Ricky."

"Not you too. Why is everyone pushing Mark on me? We're just friends."

"Because Ricky isn't right for you. The things that jerk says about you. He's ruining your reputation. You would be lucky to get a decent boy like Mark."

"You're really one to talk about reputations. You sleep with any old jerk who asks you out. Your slate isn't so clean, either."

"I'm a lot older than you, Angel, and I've been around. I don't care what people say about me. I see how Ricky treats you. No guy has ever hit me, and none of them had better try it. Everybody talks about how Ricky dogs you out so bad."

"He's not dogging me out."

"Quit kidding yourself, Angel. You're my sister, and I don't like the way he treats you. I've even talked to him about it. He just laughed, and he said you could handle yourself. I know you act so tough, but I know you, Angel. When things happen to you, you feel it hard. I know he must be hurting you."

"He won't leave me alone." I start crying, and I brush the tears away. "I've told him I want to break things off, but he said I'm not going anywhere until he's ready for me to go. You don't know what it's like. He acts as if he owns me, and I can't do anything without hearing his mouth about it. I wish he would just leave me alone."

"I tried to warn you, but you said you knew what you were doing. I've known Ricky Flecher since we were in grade school, and he's always been stuck on himself. He uses girls to make him feel good. I should know because when we were freshmen, he tried to get with me, but I wouldn't put up with his shit."

"I don't want to talk about it anymore. Even talking about Ricky depresses me. I need to drink to keep from thinking about it. That's as bad as you and the weed."

"I haven't been getting high lately. Keith has made me see what a big cop-out it is. It doesn't matter if I have problems with Mom and Dad. I don't need to stay high to keep from thinking about them."

"Keith must be some guy," I say. "You've been

smoking weed since ninth grade."

"If I can quit after all that time, you can quit drinking."

"I have tried. I've been drinking since I was nine. Remember? We tried Dad's Scotch, and we both got sick. I kept drinking off and on, but lately, I've been drinking more. Ricky makes me feel so bad, and I drink so I can feel up."

"It's just a cop-out."

"I know that. I'm not saying that it's right. I'm just trying to explain it to you."

"This is good," she says. "We should talk more."

"You're the one who never wanted to talk."

"I know," she says. "I've been blaming you for stuff that's not even your fault. You know how things were before they told me I was adopted. It was you and me against them, and we felt united because of the way they treated us. No matter how bad it got or how worthless they made us feel, at least we had each other, and that was all that mattered."

"I used to feel that way too," I say. "We used to lay here at night and talk things over. You always hated them so much, and you were the one who back-talked Dad when he gave us the beatings, and I just took them as if I was a dummy. You always stood up for us because Mom never would, and I always thought you would, but then it was like you just didn't even care anymore. Dad could do whatever he wanted, and he took that as his cue to do whatever he pleased."

"Once I found out I was adopted, I felt like I couldn't complain about anything. If my own parents didn't want me, how was I going to bitch about how the people who did take me in treat me? I felt so sorry for myself, and you weren't even my real sister, and I resented that too, but not because of them. I've always hated Mom and Dad, but it felt worse to know that you weren't really blood, and I've had trouble dealing with that ever since they told me the truth about my adoption."

"I didn't know that. I always thought you just hated me. I always tried to talk about things with you, and you just tuned me out. Remember how Mom always used to stick me on you? I knew you hated having me around, but I used to beg her to let me go with you because I felt like that was the only way I got your attention, and I could be around you some. Because you just completely turned your back on me, and I thought you just hated everything about me. I just wanted to change into how you wanted me to be so bad, but I never could be just like you no matter how I tried, and I finally just gave up."

"I never really hated you," she says. "I mostly just felt sorry for myself."

"You have so much going for you, though," I say. "I've always felt like leftover dog shit."

"You can't let a guy determine your self-worth. You need to learn to love yourself and like yourself for who you are. Nobody is ever going to build you up the way you want, and people spend all their time trying to tear you apart. Keith is great, and he's helped me a lot, but I don't depend on him for every little thing. A woman needs to be independent, or she'll never have any freedom. Most guys just like to control you anyway, because they think bossing you around is the only way they can keep you in your place."

"Ricky is the ultimate control freak," I say. "And I've been stupid for letting him treat me like that. Still, sometimes it's like I don't have any control of that either. I've been beaten down so much that it's hard to pick myself up and to know that I'm really worthwhile because I can't dust off all that self-doubt."

"You'll learn, Angel," she promises. "You're just still very much a child. You've always wanted to grow up so fast, but you weren't really ready, so it's been easy for Ricky to play on your emotions and have your feelings confused. The older you get, the easier you'll find that it is to cope with men and not let them consume your whole life. The more interests you have, the less time you have to spend devoting yourself to some guy."

"I know you're telling me some good advice, but you've been that way too," I remind her. "I've seen you clinging to a lot of guys for assurance."

"I always feel like I've dated so many jerks who remind me of Dad," she explains. "I guess unconsciously, I seek them out, or else men can see that weakness in you, and they're drawn to you."

"Dad is such a big jerk," I say. "And every time things go wrong with him at work or something, he tries to take it out on us. And Mom is such a stupid bitch, and she never stands up to him or makes him stop. They act like we have to be so perfect, and we should never make a mistake, but they fuck up all the time, and they try to act like it's our fault that things don't go the way they want them to."

"I know. Sometimes, I get so jealous of you. You're really Mom's and Dad's kid, and you don't have to worry about failing them completely. They're going to love you anyway. I feel like I need to prove myself to them. They had all their high expectations, and I was supposed to live up to them. But their standards are so outrageous, and I gave up trying to please them. Then, when things got too rough, I just ran away. Up until that time, I was under so much pressure that I thought I would snap. So, when I came back home, I just said, "fuck it," because they're never going to be happy with me, so why even try anymore?"

"Think about how I feel. You're the chosen one. Mom and Dad picked you out of all those kids. I just happened along by accident after they had given up hope. They threw all your achievements up in my face, and they expected me to measure up to you. There was no way I ever could, but I just kept on trying anyway. I am so totally jealous of you too, and I've spent half my life trying to convince Mom and Dad that I am just as good as you, so they won't feel sorry that I was even born. Maybe they do anyway because they never want to be bothered with me, and I have to beg for bits of attention. Sometimes Mom and Dad act like those stupid little crumbs they do give are so much, so forget them. I'm through trying anymore because it's too late to make up for the past, and I know they don't care how they treat me now, so why should I keep hoping in the future that things will get any better?"

"We're both hopeless, aren't we?" she asks. "Maybe it's Mom's and Dad's fault. I know it is because they never try to see how it is for us, but they expect so much out of us. They always push us so hard, and they never stop to think about how we're feeling."

"I never thought you felt the same way."

"I hide my feelings a lot too," she says. "I figure nobody would understand."

"You have so many friends, though."

"I've always had lots of friends, but never one special friend. I can't talk about myself that easily. I just smile, and I always pretend I agree with the crowd."

"I do that sometimes too. Since Jody and I stopped being friends, I haven't felt as close to anyone else. I talk to Mark a lot, but it's not the same."

Diane and I talk until dinner time. It's good to talk to my sister. I never thought we had that many things we share, but Mom and Dad are such a big problem to her too. I never even figured that, because I've always been too jealous to see her side of anything. We've been going through a lot of the same things, and I never even knew it. It's hard imagining Diane upset or scared about anything, but she has feelings too, and things get her down. I never really thought about her feeling sad about being unwanted by her birth parents. Or how she feels like she owes our parents loyalty for even taking her in. I just thought my sister was so lucky and I figured her life was a piece of cake, so that's why I was always so jealous that she got all the attention because she was the adopted one.

I've been so down on her that I never thought about how she was feeling. Now I know that she does have things difficult too. We both decide to be more understanding of each other's situation, and we are going to try to get along better. We are sisters, no matter what, and we deserve to have a relationship with each other. The most I ever hoped for was to be on speaking terms with her, so this new development is terrific, and I feel better about a lot of things.

Ricky comes over about an hour after dinner. I'm not in the mood to put up with his shit. Usually, he loves to venture into the house, so Dad can fuss over him and act like he's such a Big Shot, but he wants to stay outside now. I put on my shoes, and I go out front to talk to him. He has gone over near the Oaktree, so he can't be heard in the house, and spoil my parents' perfect perception of him. Whatever he says, I'm not going to let it get to me.

"You really like throwing it up in my face, don't you?" he demands.

"I don't know why you're talking about."

"You're fucking Davis, and you want everybody to know about it."

"Just because you're out there screwing every girl at school, don't try to put it off on me," I say. "I get so sick and tired of you jumping in my face about shit when you know you're the one who's out there whoring around."

"You're the one who's the fucking whore," he says. "Why else would anybody even want you?"

"I don't have to listen to this shit," I say.

"Well, you damn well better listen, bitch," he says. "Because if I ever find out you've screwed out on me, I'll kick your ass worse than I ever have, and there isn't shit you can do about it."

I just glare at him.

"You better wipe that look off your face before I slap you down now," he warns. "You don't want me to get really mad."

"Ricky, I don't want to fight."

"Your ass should have thought about that before now," he says. "I try my best to get along with you, but you're always starting some shit. I've told you about

Davis, but you won't listen. Do you think I'm stupid? I know how you feel about him, and you can't even deny it, so don't even bother trying to lie to me about it."

"You don't know how I feel about anything," I say. "You think you do, but you know nothing at all about me."

"I know what a little slut you are," he says. "What else is there to know?"

"All you do is call me names and put me down," I say. "At least Mark cares about me, and he treats me right, and that's what makes you so mad. You can't stand to see me happy for even five minutes."

"I'm sure he's Mr. Feel Good." Ricky sneers. "That little fag can't even keep Linda satisfied, or her ass wouldn't have to play out on him. You think I'm worried about that little punk? I already half kicked his pussy ass before, and if he crosses me again, I'll really give him something to think about. You better think about that the next time you get the urge to call him and try to play me for a fool."

"I don't know how many times I've told you - Mark and I are just friends."

"That's why you beat up his girlfriend?"

"Linda is not Mark's girlfriend anymore, and besides, she started it. I wasn't going to stand there like a dummy and do nothing."

"And I suppose Davis didn't have anything to do

with it. Bitch, I'm not stupid. You're nothing but a whore, and that's why Davis is sticking up under you. You're giving that limp dick motherfucker a blow job or something."

"I don't care what you think. I've told you the truth. If there's nothing else, I'm going into the house."

"You're damn right there's something else," he says, and he grabs my arm hard. "I've warned you before. You're not going to go around making people talk about me."

"I'm tired of hearing about your image. Nobody cares about what you do. People have other things to talk about. If I'm embarrassing you so much, you know what you can do. I don't see why you even bother with me. There are plenty of girls at school who would date you, and they would do anything for you. Why don't we just call it quits? You can see we can't get along."

Ricky digs his nails down so hard in my arm, and I try to yank it away, but he won't let go. I guess my parents don't care about our fighting. Ricky has been so mad that his voice gets loud at times. I feel like the whole neighborhood is watching, and everybody knows about my business. I care more about what people think about things than about his stupid ass. Ricky's face is so mean, and he's so angry that he shakes, but I force myself not to be so scared of him. It's not like Ricky going to beat me up in front of my house, but motherfucker does it at school, so I don't know what to think. Maybe he will just agree with me, and everything will be okay.

"Bitch, if I wanted somebody else, I would have them. There are plenty of girls who are better than you. I can have my choice of them."

I finally yank my arm out of his grip, and I rub it where it's sore, but I don't care about that. I just want to end all the real pain once and for all.

"If I'm so bad, why do you stay around?" I ask. "I'm sure I can find somebody better too."

"Bitch, please. Who do you think you're kidding? You're stupid, you can't even dress right, and you're so Goddamn ugly that all the make-up in the world isn't going to cover it up. The only good thing about you is your pussy, and that's all you have going for yourself."

"You bastard," I spit out. "I hate you so much."

"Davis isn't even going to want you after I tell him how much I've used you. Just face it - you're going to keep on being my girl for as long as I want you to, and when I'm through with you, you're not going to even be able to pay some guy for a date."

"Go to Hell!" I scream and then I run into the house. I really believe that he would tell Mark something just to keep him away. I hate Ricky so much. He may think he has got me down the way he likes and that the fight in me is still gone. Still, I remember the things Diane said about trying to love my own self and not letting some guy determine my self-worth, so I'm not going to play his games anymore. I wasn't going to go at first, but I'm so mad at Ricky that I'm going to get even with him. I'm going to call Mark and tell him that I'll go to Janice's beach party.

CHAPTER 27

I'm ready for Janice's beach party an hour before time. I'm just wearing my swimsuit. It's warm outside. They say it might get up to 98 degrees. Jody said she's only wearing a swimsuit too. She's going to let Russ take her to the beach party. She told me that Mitch already has a date with some other girl, so there won't be any problems.

I can't believe that she hasn't decided between the two of them yet. It's been almost seven months. I guess she sees something in them that she likes, and she doesn't want to make a choice. I bet it must get complicated at times. I would find it hard juggling two guys and remembering different stuff about each one of them.

When I called Jody, and I told her I would be joining them, we talked, but it wasn't like old times. I think she's being careful. I guess I really hurt her, so it's going to be hard for her to forget that. I'm willing to give her some time because I want us to be friends again. Jody's really changed over the year. I see her walking down the halls at school, and she looks like she doesn't care what anybody thinks about her. She used to look down like she couldn't look anybody in the eyes. I guess Russ and Mitch have given Jody a lot of confidence in herself.

I hope Ricky isn't there. I don't want to have him making a scene. I shouldn't care what he thinks. He said everything he had to say yesterday. He doesn't care about my feelings, he just wants me to do things his way. I'm not going to worry about it anymore and I'll go to the party and have fun with my friends.

Mark comes to the door to pick me up. Jody and Russ are already in the car. Mark's wearing cutoffs, but he has his trunks on underneath them. Mark and I are always laughing and joking around, so I know tonight will be fun. I wish it really was a date, but I'm glad to be spending some time with him. Jody and Russ both say, "Hi," then they go back to their conversation.

I talk to Mark.

"This beach party tonight should be fun," Mark says. "The band is going to be the Rift Raft."

"Sounds like fun."

"I'm glad you decided to come along," he says. "I didn't think you would."

"I'm tired of sitting at home, waiting on Ricky to call. I'm going to start doing the things I want to do."

"I'm glad to have the company. I didn't want to

be a fifth wheel tonight."

"You should start dating. There are plenty of girls who would give you a chance."

"I don't want another Linda," he says. "If there was somebody like you, I'd give it a try."

"I don't know whether to take that as a compliment or not."

"You know what I mean. You're not hung up on impressing people. You say what's on your mind. Some girls say what they think you want to hear."

"My mouth gets me in trouble sometimes."

"Hmmm."

Mark parks in the parking lot, and we pile out of the car. The spotlights are on, but the closer we get to the canteen, the darker it gets. There's a bandstand set up, and the band is warming up. There are a lot of kids crowded up close to the bandstand. The whole school was invited to this beach party, so over two thousand kids are hanging around. I know the night is going to be so exciting because Janice's beach party is the social event of the year. We manage to find a free space that's close to the pier, and Russ spreads our blanket out. He sits by Jody, and I'm close to Mark. We talk about nonsense stuff, and we say "Hi" to the people who pass that we know. Sherry comes by, and she gives me a surprised look. I smile at her, and then I introduce her to Mark and Russ because she already knows Jody.

"Do you girls want anything to drink?" Russ

asks.

“A Coke,” Jody says. “And bring me a hamburger too.”

“Just a Coke for me,” I say.

Mark and Russ go over to the canteen. There's a long line. The band has started playing, and I sway with the beat. Some kids are dancing, but mostly, everyone is just listening to music. I watch Mark. He looks sexy in his cutoffs. His legs are already tanned, and he's really built.

“How are you doing?” Jody asks.

“I'm okay.”

“Mark seems happy. I'm glad you're giving him a chance.”

“Nothing has changed. If Ricky knew I was here, there would be some trouble.”

“I don't see why you put up with that jerk.”

“Ricky thinks he owns me. He wants to tell me what to do and who I can talk to. If he could make me think the way he wants, he would do that too. He tries to control me.”

“Mitch tried to pull that shit too, but I told him I'm my own girl. I can do what I want, and he's not my boss.”

“Ricky's crazy. I mean that. He really needs some professional help. But let's not talk about that. Let's talk about you. Give me the latest."

"There hasn't been that much happening. My parents are okay, and they're getting along great. I'm seeing Mitch and Russ. I'm glad school is almost over because this summer I'm going to stay with my Aunt Jenny in Indianapolis. "

"Without your parents?" I ask, surprised. "I thought you were afraid to leave them."

"I'm not scared of them leaving me anymore. I met Aunt Jenny at Thanksgiving, and she's great. She's a doctor and everything. She doesn't have any kids, so she asked Suzy if I could go up and spend Summer Vacation with her."

"That sounds like fun," I say. "I'll probably have a boring summer."

"You have to keep me up on what Mitch and Russ are doing, so we'll keep in touch with each other."

"Don't rub it in, Jody." Russ hands Jody her drink and burger. "What am I going to do without you for three months?"

"I'm sure you'll think of something."

"What are you doing this summer, Angel?" Mark asks me.

"Same as always." I take a sip of my drink. "Laying around the house and watching Soap Operas."

"I got a job at the playground near my house," Russ says. "I've been working there since I was thirteen."

"Mr. Cox got me a job cutting grass," Mark says. "I don't mean any kid stuff. I'll be doing acres on this power mower. It's just 'til football practice starts in July."

Russ and Jody go down to the bandstand to be closer to the band. Mark suggests that we go swimming. He takes off his cutoffs, and we head towards the water. We do a couple of laps, and then we start playing around in the water. Mark goes underwater, and he doesn't come back up. About a minute goes by, and I start getting worried. I don't know what's happening until I'm pulled underwater too. I come up spitting water and wiggling to be free. Mark's lips brush against mine, and I look at him in surprise. He tries to laugh it off, but I wish he would kiss me again.

We don't come out of the water until over an hour later. Jody and Russ are still up near the bandstand. Russ has his arm around her, and he's holding her tight. I dry off, and then I hand the towel to Mark. He dries off while I stare at him. His wet trunks show it all, and he catches me watching him. He starts laughing, and I pretend I find something interesting at the canteen. We're just sitting there talking when Ricky comes along.

"Look at the lovebirds," he says. Ricky stops right in front of us, and he's sneering. I don't want any trouble. I should have known things were going too well. I bet he thinks Mark and I are out on a date, and

I'm two-timing him. He's stepped out plenty of times, but I'm supposed to take it. Now, he's caught me alone with another guy, and his ego is hurt.

"Do you have a problem?" Mark asks Ricky.

"You're the one with the problem. You can't even keep your own girlfriend happy, but you go after my leftovers."

"Ricky, will you just leave us alone?" I ask. "I don't want any trouble."

"You should have thought about that before you showed up here with that punk," Ricky says.

"Angel can see anybody she wants to," Mark says. "You don't own her."

"As long as I'm fucking her, I'll tell her who she can see. And it damn sure won't be another guy."

"I'm here with Jody and Russ," I explain. "Mark just came along."

"You don't have to explain anything, Angel," Mark says.

"Angel, get your things and come on," Ricky orders. "You're going home with me."

"Angel isn't going anywhere with you," Mark tells him. "She's here with me, and she's going to stay at this beach party for as long as she wants. Unless you want to start something, you can just get lost."

"Yeah, I'm starting something."

Mark jumps up, and Ricky gets in his face. They start talking about each other, and I know it's more than about me. It's like they hate each other for something else, and they're just using me as an excuse to have a confrontation. Things get out of hand, and I know it's going to lead to a fight. I try to break them apart, but Ricky slaps me so hard that I fall onto the sand. That's when Mark punches him in the mouth. People start gathering around. I feel so embarrassed and absolutely useless. I know Mark is doing what he thinks is right, but I'm scared that Ricky is going to hurt him.

The next thing I know, Ricky is on the ground, and Mark is on top of him. Mark keeps punching Ricky in the stomach and stuff. Ricky fights back, but it's apparent that Mark is getting the best of him. The band has even stopped playing, and it's like the two of them are the most important things, and nobody cares about anything else.

"Stop it!" Janice screams. "You're ruining my party!"

Mark just keeps on hitting Ricky. He's not fighting back anymore, but it's like Mark doesn't even care. Some guys pull Mark away, and he struggles to get free. I've never seen that look in his eyes before. Ricky gets up, holding his stomach, and he looks like a scared kid. He appears like a different person when he's not wearing the cocky, superior smile. I almost feel sorry for him, but I'm glad somebody finally hurt him like he's hurt me all these months. I feel good that it was Mark who came to my defense, because I finally believe that everybody was right, and he does have feelings for me.

"If you ever touch Angel again, I'll kill your ass. I don't give a damn who you are. It's over, man. You just better get that through your head," Mark tells Ricky.

"Are you all right, Angel?" Jody asks.

I'm too upset to talk. I just nod.

"We can leave if you want to. Russ and I don't mind. We can go over to my house."

"Thanks, Jody."

Jody takes Russ's hand, and they head towards the car. I fold up the blanket, and I wait on Mark as he finally calms down. He comes over to me, and his face isn't messed up. I tell him about going over to Jody's house, and he puts his arm around me. People stare at us as we start walking away. I hold Mark tighter. I feel safe for once.

"Mark, do you really want to go over to Jody's house?"

"I'll do whatever you say."

"I want to be with you. I know I shouldn't make the first move, but that's how I feel."

Mark searches my face, and then he says, "You don't owe me nothing."

“I know that. I love you, and I want to make love to you.”

“I love you too, but I don't want to rush anything.”

“We're not rushing. We've lost too much time. Now, I want things to be right. I don't want to wait any longer.”

“As long as you're sure.”

“I'm sure.”

I feel so happy that I could cry. Everything is going to be all right. Ricky can't touch me anymore, and I know Mark loves me. I'm only sorry I wasted so much time. I remember our kiss, and I know everything else is going to be just as good.

CHAPTER 28

Mark drives around a while before he tries to find us a Hotel. We talk some, but mostly there's silence. The radio is on, and I listen to music. Mark finally parks by Pop Tofflers. He turns towards me, and I can see the concern written all over his face.

"Are you sure you really want to do this?" he asks. "I know how much he's hurt you."

"I love you, Mark. I want to be with you. It doesn't have anything to do with Ricky Flecher."

"I'm not like him."

"I know that."

"I want you and everything, but I can wait until it's all right."

"It's right now. I should have told you how I felt a long time ago, but I didn't. We wasted so much time when we could have been together and happy, so I don't want to waste any more of it. That's why I don't want to put this off any longer."

"I love you, Angel."

"I love you too."

The Hotel he finds, Pine Oaks, is almost out of town. Mark goes in to register, and I sit in the car. I hope he doesn't have a hard time getting the room. It's funny, but I'm a little scared. After all I've been through with Ricky, I shouldn't have any fears at all, but it's different for Mark. I never cared about how sex was with Ricky. I want this to be special. I love Mark, and I want everything to be all right.

"The guy wanted an extra ten bucks, or he wouldn't let us have the room."

"What a jerk."

"It's room 43."

We walk towards room 43. It's not that large. Just a bed and a television. There's a Bible on top of the TV set, but it hasn't had much use. I sit on the mattress, and Mark sits down beside me. He looks nervous. I know he's been with Linda and everything, but he doesn't seem to know what to do.

"You're okay, aren't you? I didn't bring anything."

"I'm on The Pill."

"We have the room until noon tomorrow."

"It's okay for you to stay all night, isn't it?"

"Yeah. You won't get in trouble, will you?"

"No. I'll just tell them I spent the night with Jody."

"I'll be back."

Mark goes into the bathroom. I take off my swimsuit, and I slip under the covers. The light is on, but I don't turn it off. I'm not embarrassed about Mark seeing me naked. It takes about twenty minutes for him to come back, and I'm just about ready to go see what's wrong with him when he comes out of the bathroom. He takes a cigarette out of the pack in his back pocket, and he lights up. I sit up, and I look at him.

"What's wrong, Mark?"

"Nothing."

"Don't I turn you on?"

"Sure - it's not that."

"What is it then?"

"Linda is the only girl I ever had sex with, and it only happened once." Mark starts blushing. "I didn't feel right about having sex with her."

"What about all that stuff you told me?"

"That was only some talk. I didn't want you to think I was a big jerk. My father's a preacher, and all that guilt shit was drilled into me when I was young.

When my parents found out about me having sex with Linda, my dad really gave me a big hassle about it. After we broke up, that bitch told them she was pregnant by me, so my parents would know I'd had sex with her, but there was no way I was a daddy because it had been nine months since I had touched her. Linda was just lying about the pregnancy anyway, and she just wanted to cause some trouble."

"I wouldn't do anything like that."

"I know that. You don't know how hard it is to be a preacher's kid. I can't do anything wrong without getting a sermon about it."

"My father's like that too," I tell him. "Don't let your father get you down."

"You just don't know what he's like. Always doing stupid shit in God's name and embarrassing me to death. Maybe that's why I'm always fucking up. I want to show people that I'm nothing like him, and I always end up looking like an asshole."

"You're not an asshole, Mark," I say softly. "You're the sweetest guy I've ever known, and that's why I love you so much."

"You're not as tough as you pretend to be either, and that's why I love you," he says. "I just want to be able to please you. I've had some trouble in the past, you know, getting it up and I couldn't handle it if I failed with you too. Linda always made me feel so stupid, and she really made me feel like a little boy when she told me she had been screwing Ricky the whole time we were together."

"That bitch!"

"Yeah. Well, how do you think I felt?" Mark asks. "That's why if you want, we can just lie here and watch TV and talk some. It wouldn't bother me if you didn't even want to try."

"I'm going to do more than try, Mark," I promise. "When you really love somebody, it's different, and you're not under the same pressure. I'm going to make you forget Linda ever existed, and nobody is ever going to hurt you again."

"I didn't just fail with Linda," he says sadly. "I haven't been able to be with any girls."

"No more talking," I say. "There's time enough for that later. Ricky may have been awful to me, but I know I learned how to please a guy."

Mark finishes his second cigarette, and he sits next to me. I let the sheet fall away, and I take his face in my hands. I kiss him as hard as I can, feeling like it's the second kiss I ever really enjoyed, and my mouth just melts on his, giving me such a dizzy feeling. I know it never has to end. Mark keeps increasing the pressure of his lips too, and it's not long before he's French-kissing me back. For once, I'm glad for all my sexual experience. I don't try to rush him. I kiss him for a while, and I know where to touch him. I just want him to lose himself in the moment and forget everything else. In a way, it's like we're two virgins just discovering sex for the first time. Ricky made it so awful for me, and I never even wanted to admit that it was happening to me, and the only thing there was my body. Mark feels so guilty anyway, and that bitch, Linda, just used that to make him feel worse about himself, so I don't blame him for being so scared and thinking he's always going to fail. It's not long before he really gets into it, and it's about both of us, not just me getting up his confidence. Mark knows how to get me hot, too, so his touches just set me on fire, and I've never been so wet before in my life. I can feel his hard-on pressing against my leg, and I pull him down on top of me.

"Angel, I don't know what to say."

"Don't talk."

I kiss him again, and I push my tongue inside his mouth, and I dart it back and forth. I want him in me so bad, so I spread my legs open, and I'm the one who guides him inside me. It feels so exciting, and I know Mark is getting pleasure, too, because he gasps out loud. I always knew it could feel good, and I was only dead down there because I could feel no passion for Ricky. Suddenly, it is so alive, and it's like every nerve in my body is centered on that one spot, and the more I move against Mark, the more intense the feelings get. I meet his every thrust, and maybe I get too wild, and I make too much noise. Still, it's like every part of my being is finally free, and I just want to let out a howler in joy, because Mark is mine and he loves me, and he knows how to fuck the shit out of me. It's different than it was with Ricky, though. Mark makes love to me too, and he takes his time about it, sucking on my tits and kissing my neck, and he makes sure I'm feeling something also. I love him so much, and I knew it had to be terrific between us. Once he gets over his fears, and I give into my passion, the magic just starts. I have the first orgasm of my life, and all my shaking makes Mark cum soon after. Afterward, I give him a big hug, and I lay my head on his chest.

"God, I'm so happy," I say. "You've done so much for me."

"I'm just starting."

"Was it this good with Linda?" I ask, anyway. "I mean, the one time you actually did it. Did you make her come and have her screaming for more?"

"What made you ask that?"

"I was just wondering. It wasn't this way with Ricky. I just laid there, and I didn't feel anything."

"Did you feel anything just now?" he asks. "I hope you weren't just acting like that to build up my confidence."

"Mark, I would never fake it with you," I tell him.

"I wasn't sure," he says. "Sometimes, I think all girls lie, and they tell you the shit that you want to hear, but I want us to always be honest with each other."

“We always will be from now on.”

“Did I really get to you?” he asks. “You really felt something?”

“Yeah, a lot of things.”

“I guess it's different when you love somebody,” he says. “You forget about yourself and your hang-ups, and you try harder to please that person.”

“You always please me. You make me feel like I really matter. You don't try to put me down and make me feel like I'm stupid. Ricky came from an affluent family and he ruled Central, and he was a part of that uppity “in” group. Since I was so poor and never good enough for them, he always acted like he had to tell me what to do. I don't even know why Ricky kept me around for so long. All he ever wanted to do was use me for sick-ass sex, and if he wasn't hurting me that way, he had to kick my ass in front of everybody else and harm me in another way. Most of the time, I just felt like leftover dog shit, and I couldn't even imagine anybody decent as you cared about me.”

“I'm not going to put you down, and I will never let anybody else ever hurt you again. Don't let that motherfucker win. You're special, and none of that matters to me, and I don't care about any of that. I love you the way you are. You don't try to put on any pretense. Linda was such a phony. She always made me feel like she only loved me because I kept on excelling at sports, and if I wasn't such a jock, she would have dumped me a long time ago. Fuck her. All I ever did was spend money I couldn't afford on her and try my best to please her when I never could. Linda never even wanted me in the first place, and nothing I did was ever going to be good enough for her, because she was a rich Honey Bear. All I ever was going to be was a poor ass white boy from the wrong part of town."

"Let's not talk about Linda and Ricky anymore. They're out of our lives, and they're not important."

"Okay."

"Are you sleepy?"

"A little."

"Me too."

"Do you want to watch TV?"

"No. I just want to lie here. I'm afraid I'm going to wake up and find out this is all a dream."

"You're going to wake up in my arms and realize how real it is."

"Mmmmmmmm." I kiss his chest. "Hold me tighter."

Mark turns out the light, and he wraps his arms around me. I feel so close to him. We lie in the dark. It's not that long before Mark falls asleep. There's a little wheezing sound, but he doesn't really snore. I'm too excited to sleep because I've never been so happy. Finally, all of my dreams have come true. He doesn't know it yet, but Mark Davis is never getting away from me. I love him with my whole heart, and I always get what I really want.

"I love you, Mark," I whisper in his ear. "We'll be together always and always."

I snuggle even closer to him, and I feel content just to lie there and watch him sleep, but my eyes keep getting heavy, and I know it's not going to be long before I drift off too.

CHAPTER 29

When I get home the next night, I see my father sitting on the porch, smoking his pipe. I can see by his face that he is furious, and I know I'm in for another one of his scenes.

I'm not going to let it ruin the happiness I feel after my day with Mark. I go on past him, and I walk into the house. Mom jumps up and comes over to me. She looks like she's really been worrying.

"Where have you been, Angel?" she asks. "We've been worried sick."

"Over to Jody's house," I lie.

"That's a lie! I called over there, and her mother said she hasn't seen you in months," Dad informs me. "I want to know where you've been."

"I told you. Over Jody's," I insist.

Dad slaps me hard, and I grab my face. I hear Mom's sharp gasp, but she doesn't try to stop him. She never does anything when he hits us, and that's why he does it so much. He just keeps on abusing me, but I don't try to fight back. I refuse to let the tears come. When he sees that he's not going to get to me that way, he stops.

"Now, you better tell me where you've been."

"I've been with Mark. Last night we made love, and it was beautiful. I'm not going to let you and Mom make our lovemaking into something dirty that I should be ashamed about. I love Mark so much, and I'm going to keep on seeing him."

I run towards my room.

My parents make me so sick. When I needed them, they were never there, but as soon as it looks like there's going to be some happiness in my life, they start acting like the concerned parents. I don't care what they think about me. Their opinions no longer matter to me. They're my parents, but I don't know if I love them.

We get into a lot of fights after that. I say a lot of things to them when I'm mad that I know I don't mean. Then I go up to my room, and I cry. I accuse them of all sorts of things that I know I don't believe. I just want to hurt them as much as they hurt me. Sometimes, I feel so bad that all I want to do is die.

My parents don't approve of my relationship with Mark. They know we make love and they say that's the only reason Mark wants me. Dad talks about me like I'm a slut, but Mom never says anything to defend me. Maybe she agrees with him. They treated Mark so bad when he came over that he doesn't even come in the house anymore. He just sits in the car, and he blows. Dad has something to say about that too.

Sometimes, they make me so mad that all I want to do is scream. Mom and Dad do stupid things like come upstairs and tell me I've left something lying around downstairs. They couldn't bring it up, no way, but they can come up and tell me about it. Dad complains about my clothes, but he won't buy me any new things. There is nothing outlandish or weird about what I wear. I can't do anything right. They always say they are right and insist that I'm wrong.

Finally, they found out the truth about me being expelled at school. I was just going to hide it when I was supposed to go to Central next fall, and pretend I was attending classes the first semester of the school year but spend all that time hanging out at Northland Mall. The only reason I didn't get punished this year was that the fight happened on a Friday, and Finals were occurring the next week, so school was almost over. A whole month has passed since then, and so it's even too late to punish me over something that happened so long ago. I feel like my parents are just using anything to bitch at me about, and they needed another excuse to complain.

Now, they are on my case about going to our church, First Church of Christ, every Sunday. I believe in God and everything, but I have never liked going to church. Now, they think I'm so immoral that I need a good preaching to. Reverend Sanderson is so far behind it. He's always saying, "Be not of the world. God wants us to give up all the worldly things and just concentrate on him." What a hypocrite. He's the one who's driving around in the new Cadillac.

My parents are always saying if I don't go to church, they won't let me see Mark anymore. That's the threat they use all the time. They know they can't take anything else away from me and make me hurt so badly. Sometimes, I feel like running away or something. I can't stand living in this house. If I knew Mark would go with me, I'd be gone in a second.

I never tell Mark how I'm feeling. He knows they'll never like him, so he doesn't worry about it. But it hurts me to see that they are against the one person who makes me feel happy. They accepted Ricky Flecher like he was significant, and he did me like a dog. Mark treats me so exceptional, and it's like my parents can't stand it. The fighting and fighting keep going on, and I just want it to stop.

When Mark comes to pick me up on Friday night, I put on a smile, and I act like there's nothing wrong with me. Mark drives to Cassidy's. We sit on the car hood, and we talk. Mark has a six-pack of beer, and we drink them. There's nothing much going on around us. Things don't start picking up until about midnight. The radio is on, and I sway with the beat.

"Angel, what's wrong?" Mark asks.

"Nothing. Why did you ask?"

"You've been acting funny lately."

"Maybe it's because we haven't made out since Tuesday night."

"Are you suggesting something?"

"Yeah, this sure isn't exciting."

There's more to us than a physical attraction, but holding each other is important too. We go out on dates, and I go over to Mark's house sometimes. I don't care how bad things can get for him at home, they never let anything show when I'm there, and I'm grateful for that. His parents treat me great. They make me feel like part of the family, and they act happy that their son has somebody that is finally going to treat him right, and that's the only thing that matters to them. I like going over there. It's nice to see a family that loves each other no matter what they go through, and they do things together besides fight. I know they're not perfect, and maybe nobody's family really is, but anything is better than what I'm forced to go through daily. I handle the problem in the same old stupid way. I don't care if drinking is a cop-out, you need to do whatever it takes to get you through the hard times, and besides Mark, that's the only thing that can make me feel better.

"Hey, kids! Break it up!"

Somebody starts banging on the window. Mark starts cussing the guy out until he sees that he's a cop.

We weren't doing anything wrong, but I get scared anyway, and I wonder what's up.

Mark opens the door, and he steps out of the car. It's a while before I follow him. We stand by the side of the car and my blouse is buttoned crooked. I don't fix it. I'm embarrassed. I'm not wearing a bra, and the cop saw me with my top open. I only hope he didn't get an eyeful of Mark sucking on my tits. At least we hadn't taken it any farther than that yet.

We're not the only ones getting hassled. There are about five patrol cars parked near Baskin Robbins, and there are kids in the back of four of them. Mark locks the vehicle, and the cop leads us over to the fifth patrol car. Mark is pissed, and he starts bitching at the police. I'm mad too, but I'm too scared to say anything. My knees are shaking, and I think I'm going to pass out or worse yet, throw up.

It's not that far to the Police Station, but to me, it feels like a million miles, and I get more upset as time goes by because things are bad enough at home, but now it's going to get ten times worse. We don't find out what we're getting booked about until after we get there. Great, I'm going to get grounded for the rest of my life, because I've been arrested for Trespassing at a Shopping Center! I really feel like being sick now.

We can't leave until after our parents pick us up. I'm not in too big of a hurry to call Dad. I know he'll yell, and he'll blame Mark for getting me arrested. I let Mark call his folks first. He left his car back there, and

I want to put off a confrontation as long as possible. The line is busy. I give it a try. Dad answers, and when I tell him where I'm at, he doesn't even seem surprised. It's like he wouldn't put anything past me. Dad just says that he'll be down.

That worries me more. I know how Dad gets when he holds back his anger. When we get home, he'll throw a big tantrum, and he'll probably end up beating me up. I go sit back beside Mark, and my boyfriend sees how upset I am. He puts his hand on my knee, and he gives it a squeeze. It should make me feel better, but I know how Dad is. If I'm lucky, he'll just preach for hours.

When Dad shows up, the Desk Sergeant says, "Angel shouldn't be at Cassidy's after 11:00 p.m. The Shopping Mall is private property, and we pick up any loiters."

"Don't you worry," Dad says. "She's not going to be anywhere, because she's getting grounded for a month!"

Everybody looks over at my red face with amusement. Of course, Dad would embarrass me in front of strangers. It is bad enough that I got taken to the Police Station in the first place, but he had to go and do that. Does he think I like being arrested? Is it so much fun for me? Can't he see how scared I am? No, he just goes out of his way to make everything worse.

Dad gets a look at Mark. He stares at how tight his jeans are and then at his long hair. His face turns stone cold, and I can see all the hatred in his eyes. Dad marches over, and he stands in front of Mark. Mark just looks at him, and I just feel uncomfortable because I don't want Dad to give one of his scenes.

"You ought to be ashamed - getting my daughter arrested," he starts. Then he goes on by saying he knows what we were doing because of my blouse, and Dad says that Mark only uses me for sex, but I'm too stupid to realize that he only wants me for one thing. Dad is talking loud, and I'm so mad because he says a lot of other mean shit too, but I'm able to stay calm long as I know Mark does love me no matter what Dad says, and I know he will always be there for me.

Mark turns beet-red, and then the color drains out of his face. I know Mark, and I know he's furious. He looks like he's holding back a fury of words. Dad just keeps fussing on and on, and I know that Mark is really pissed off. For a moment, I wish that he would just pop Dad in the mouth or something, but Mark knows he's my father, and Mark needs to show him some respect, even if Dad is acting like a big asshole.

Dad finally decides to leave. I kiss Mark anyway, and he tells me to take it easy. I don't say anything to Dad in the car. I'll never forgive him for treating Mark like that. It's bad enough that they give me a scene every night, but he didn't have any right to talk to Mark like that. And I'm so mad that he tries to treat my relationship with Mark like I'm just a big slut, and that's the only reason Mark even wants to be with me. When I get into the house, Mom acts like she was worried, and she tries to hug me. I yank away, and then I go up to my room. I don't need her phony show of emotion.

I just want to be a carefree teenager. You know, go out with my friends and just hang out, date Mark and love him the way I feel, go to parties and have a lot of fun, and just become a regular teenager who doesn't have so many stupid problems. Mostly, I just want to be free to live the way I choose. I know long as I live under my parents' roof, I will never have that freedom I want. I just need to look forward to things getting even worse around here instead of anything getting any better. I get out the bottle of Vodka from under my bed, and I turn on my stereo, wanting to hear some exciting music to drown out my depressing thoughts.

Selisa Lyn Johnson

BOOKS BY THIS AUTHOR

Family Ties

Shy, socially awkward Julia Walker has been beaten into submission at the hands of her abusive stepfather. However, all this starts to change after she gets involved with Charlie Scott. Having him in her life begins to help Julia push away all the memories of the hurtful encounters with her stepfather and helps her blossom socially. But will becoming sexually active with Charlie make her relationship with him better? Or will it make her lose him? These doubts continuously linger in her mind as Julia rushes into Charlie's arms and hopes for the best, knowing love doesn't make everything perfect, but what else matters?

Long Way From Home

It's like my life is already over because I am 17 and unsure who's my unborn baby's father. My only option to get back in control of my life was to go to the Evansville Christian Girls Home. I think it will be easy just to give my baby away, and I guess I'll just have to lay around The Home for the next six months. Even though nobody understands my decision, I think I can go through with my adoption plans. At first, things go as planned, but now halfway through my pregnancy, it's like things suddenly become real, and the baby starts working its way into my heart. Can I block everything else out and go on with the plans I have for my life?

Nobody's Perfect

Fifteen-year-old Amanda Howards is one of the prettiest girls at her high school. She's become the first black Honey Bear, an elite cheerleader squad for the cutest and sexiest girls at Central. Amanda recently started dating the handsome varsity basketball player, Ed Hammer, which grants her even more popularity at school. Seeking to be perfect like the Supermodels she idolizes, Amanda starts extreme dieting. Constantly, Amanda tries to overcome her bad feelings of being an outsider on the Honey Bear squad and get closer to her childhood friend, Reesie. Will the other Honey Bears ever accept her and treat her as unique as she deserves? Will Reesie's jealousy after failing to become a Honey Bear

negatively affect their friendship? Is Amanda willing to give up Ed because he relentlessly pressures her for sex because she wants to remain a virgin? Will Amanda ever become the perfect teenager she dreams about?

Saying It Don't Make It So

Sonny is 14, but he's involved with a 20-year-old woman. The affair is addictive, turning his world around. Sonny is a pretty boy and very popular with the girls around his Projects complex. Despite this, he feels an emptiness and longs for something more. Randy Finche, his best friend, is the exact opposite. Riding on Sonny's popularity, he is constantly caught up in the Hit it and Quit it approach and urges Sonny to be more like him. Sonny resists and stays involved with Sharon Miller, which changes things drastically. When his momma learns of the affair, she is devastated but can't change his mind. Things spiral out of control, and with tensions rising, Sonny wants his life back, but Sharon's grip is too firm. If he ended it, would it be possible for him to regain his momma's trust and restore his friendship with Randy to the way it was? Is being with Sharon enough when everybody is against them?

Something I Should Know

After leaving New York, it's been hard adjusting to my new life and knowing I left all my old friends behind. I moved to Carsonville right before high school because my mother now decides to be near her parents, who she hasn't seen since she ran away fifteen years ago. Being a mixed kid with a black mother and white father, I worry about getting shunned when I go to school, even if I look white. Everybody at school only cares about popularity, especially my new friend, Angel Moore, and she pushes me to be that way too. My main obstacle to popularity is these girls in my English class who treat me like I'm a skank, and I try to ignore their verbal abuse. At home, things go up and down with my parents. Sometimes I'm trying to break away, and I want them to hold me close other times. It's like things have changed so much since we moved to Carsonville, and I'm still trying to figure it all out. In high school, everything seems so different, and I'm struggling to keep a grip on things. What happens when I can no longer do that?

Under The Gun

Being 16 and a freshman already makes me feel out of place with the rest of my class. It doesn't help that my father set the schoolyard on fire this past summer, protesting some books in the school library. I am a varsity football player, dating Linda Thomas, a beautiful and popular Honey Bear cheerleader, and looking forward to a great school year. But, crushingly, my father's religious antics that day outweigh all my successes as a jock. Trying to cope with the constant embarrassment pushes me to be a class clown. The only time I feel in control is when I'm on the ball field. So, longingly, how do I deal with the rest of my time?

When The Laughs Stop

Confident, outgoing Trey Burrows finds himself unsure and standoffish after transferring to Central High School. He went to a predominantly black high school like Lincoln High School. Trey now feels alone and lonely trying to adapt to life at Central with primarily white students. Adding to his frustration, his father's grocery store, Burrows Market, is being run out of business by a supermarket, Benny's Buy-A-Lot. Trey's cousin, Marques Wilkerson, seems to be adjusting better at Central, starring on the Boys Varsity Basketball team and being super popular from his skill on the court. However, Trey tires of basking in Marques's glory, and he worries that he will always be behind him. Can Trey keep his jealousy down and just be there for Marques? Does Burrows Market stand a chance against Benny's Buy'A-Lot?